OPERATION LUNA

JOURNEY INTO SPACE

VOLUME ONE

OPERATION LUNA

by
Charles Chilton

fantom
publishing

First published in 1954 by Herbert Jenkins Ltd, and
republished in 1958 by Pan Books Ltd

This edition published in hardback in 2011 and
in paperback in 2012 by Fantom Films
fantomfilms.co.uk

Based on the BBC radio serial *Journey into Space* first broadcast in 1953

A catalogue record for this book is available from the British Library.

Paperback Edition ISBN: 978-1-78196-024-0

Typeset by Phil Reynolds Media Services, Leamington Spa
Printed by MPG Biddles Limited, King's Lynn

Jacket design by Stuart Manning

Contents

Foreword

When Charles Chilton's wife, Penny, asked me to write a foreword for this first volume in a reprinted edition of all three *Journey into Space* novels, I couldn't have been more flattered. There was certainly no need for her to say, "Orders must be obeyed without question at all times"! These immortal words are a quote from the second part of the *Journey into Space* trilogy: *The Red Planet*. They were spoken by Whitaker, the zombie-like character who had been taken over by Martians and planted amongst the crew of the British expedition to Mars to sabotage the mission, thus preventing life on Mars being discovered.

By the time Whitaker's monotone voice was scaring audiences weekly, I was a totally committed fan of Charles Chilton and space exploration. My addiction to *Journey into Space* had begun the previous autumn (1953) when my family sat down on Monday nights at 7:30pm to listen to the BBC Light Programme's science fiction radio serial. The TV, the box with pictures, was yet to dominate our living rooms. The soaps we listened to were *Mrs Dale's Diary* and *The Archers*; our quiz shows were *Top of the Form* for schools and Wilfred Pickles' *Have a Go* (to win thirty-two shillings and sixpence

1

with a chance at the Jackpot on Mabel's table), while thrills were provided by detective Paul Temple and Special Agent Dick Barton. But the nearest we got to space was Billy Cotton's band playing while Alan Breeze sang 'Two Little Men in a Flying Saucer'.

Then suddenly, quite out of the blue, came the futuristic *Journey into Space*. For eighteen weeks until the spring, audiences were transfixed once greeted by its ethereal signature tune. It was the last serial on 'the wireless' to command a following of tens of millions.

Like many people at the time we didn't have a television. We did get one later that year thanks to a legacy from a distant relative, but its acquisition made no difference to the family's enjoyment of *Journey into Space*. The TV stayed well and truly switched off on Monday evenings, proving a point that Charles would make to me fifty years later. As I said, TV was just coming into fashion. One day Charles was confronted by a cocky TV producer, extolling the virtue of the new medium for drama. He was unwise enough to say to Charles words to the effect, "Radio is dead," then tried to rub it in with, "Tell me something you could do on radio I couldn't do better on television?" It was an idle boast and led to one of the best put-downs ever – the next episode of *Journey into Space* took place entirely in the dark when time-travellers hijacked the spacecraft's electrical power just before our intrepid explorers, Jet, Lemmy, Doc and Mitch, were due to take off to return to Earth from the Moon. Listeners were left wondering if they were about to breathe their last when their oxygen ran out with the familiar "To be continued next week..." The suspense was agonising if you were aged eleven.

I don't know who that smart-ass producer was, but I'm sure his contributions to drama haven't been as imaginative, scientifically accurate, enduring, or as wide-ranging as Charles Chilton's. How many people have on their CV a sci-fi classic, a Western comic strip (*Riders of the Range*, on the inside pages of Dan Dare's legendary *Eagle*) and a West End/Hollywood musical (*Oh! What a Lovely War*)? The latter was probably the most poignant anti-First World War film ever made, no doubt because Charles never knew his own father as he went off to the trenches never to return. It's not just my opinion but that of a lot of others too, judging by the cast of stars who were prepared to accept bit parts just to be in the film.

Speaking of actors, one of my most treasured possessions is a first edition, dust-jacketed, hardback copy of *Journey into Space: Operation Luna*, signed by the original radio cast. Charles' signature was the last to be added when we became friends because of Beagle 2, my Mars mission. Charles came to Beagle 2's rocket launch and the party when it was released from the European Space Agency's orbiter, Mars Express, to begin its descent to the planet's surface. I also invited Prince Andrew as guest of honour to the latter event at the Royal Geographical Society. It had been arranged that the project team and the regular guests would come into the building from Exhibition Road leaving the main entrance on Kensington Gore exclusively for the Royal Party. At the appointed arrival time, the official welcoming committee assembled to be introduced to His Royal Highness just inside the door. Right on cue it burst open and in walked Charles and Penny. I'm sure the Duke of York won't mind me saying that on that particular occasion the author of *Journey into Space* was the real royalty, and there were lots of people there who wanted the chance to shake Charles by the hand.

Read and enjoy this masterpiece just as I did all those years ago. It's still as fresh as ever.

Colin Pillinger
July 2011

Chapter 1
SHOCK

November 20th, 1965. The first shock came just after we had completed the circuit round the Moon. We were almost at the point where it was necessary to cut in the motors for a short burst, just powerful enough to take us out of the free orbit round the Earth's satellite and set us on a course for home.

On Jet Morgan's orders, we had taken up our places on the take-off couches. The little televiewer poised less than two feet above my face showed a sharp picture of the pitted surface of the Moon's southern hemisphere as it slowly unrolled beneath us. Little more than half-way up the screen, sharply defined against the black lunar sky, was the curved horizon. Any moment now, like a rising sun, the Earth would appear above it.

"There she is." It was Mitch, our engineer, who saw her first.

"You sound as though you haven't seen her in years," said Jet.

"I feel like I haven't."

Jet didn't pursue the conversation any further. "Position, Lemmy?"

"Coming into centre, five degrees."

"Stabiliser, Doc."

"Stabiliser," I repeated and pressed the button. The low hum of the big gyro filled the ship and gradually the Earth moved into the centre of the televiewer screen.

"Stand by to switch in motor."

"OK," said Mitch. " I – hey, wait a minute!"

"Huh? What's the matter?"

"The fuel, there's hardly any left."

"What?" The shock we all felt was clearly reflected in Jet's voice.

"But you told me there was plenty, oodles of it, you said."

"Well there's not now. Something's gone wrong. We've lost it somewhere."

"Three degrees," said Lemmy, apparently unconcerned.

Jet ignored him. "Then we must have used up much more than you estimated," he said to Mitch.

"But we couldn't have done, not on a Moon take-off. We shouldn't have used half of it."

"Two degrees."

"Have we got enough to set us on course for Earth?"

"Just about, but no more."

"Then stand by to fire the motor."

"Standing by," said Mitch.

"One degree."

"Contact !"

The ship shook as the powerful motor sprang to life. Speed began to increase, and with it the gravitational pressure. I looked up at the televiewer to see how we were doing. The Earth had drifted slightly out of centre but was now coming back into it again. By the time we had reached maximum speed we were pointing straight towards the globe, and the Moon's surface was no longer visible.

"Cut the motor," ordered Jet.

The ship ceased to tremble. Gravityless conditions returned and Lemmy heaved an audible sigh of relief.

"Course correct," he said.

"Cut the stabiliser, Doc."

I cut it, and once more, but for the pulsating of the televiewer and the hum of the power packs, silence fell upon our tight little cabin.

"Lemmy, call up base and let me know the moment you get them."

"Right." Lemmy pressed a switch above his bunk and his control panel slid back into its stowage position in the wall, automatically disconnecting itself from the main circuit as it did so. He unfastened his safety straps and half climbed, half floated down the ladder which led from his bunk to the floor, his magnetic boots making metallic clicks as he descended. I had already unfastened my straps and was putting on my boots when Jet's next order was given.

"Better check with those fuel gauges, Mitch. Make sure the fault isn't with them."

"Too right I will." Mitch made his way towards the engineering control panel.

Now Lemmy's voice could be heard calling Earth. "Hullo, Luna calling. Calling Control. Come in please."

The loudspeaker spluttered and hissed. Two seconds later the voice of Control came up from Earth.

"Hullo, Luna. Luna City calling. Standing by."

"I've got 'em, Jet," called Lemmy, but it was hardly necessary; Jet was already at his elbow.

"Morgan here. We've completed our circuit, have taken numerous photographs and are now heading back to Earth. We expect to be within landing distance in four and a half days from now."

"Thank you, Luna. What did the other side of the Moon look like?"

"Much the same as this side, except that there's a crater there, a large crater. Much bigger than you can see from Earth. It's colossal."

"Is that all?" There was a note of humour in Control's voice. "No green-eyed monsters or anything?"

Jet laughed. "No, no green-eyed monsters. Look, we have to make our routine checks now and we'll all be pretty busy for a bit. We'll call you again in two hours."

"Right. And while you're coasting home you'd better get all the rest you can."

"Huh? What for?"

"Because you're certainly going to get a big reception when you get here. I think every Prime Minister in the Commonwealth intends flying out to greet you when you land."

"Blimey!" The interjection came from Lemmy. He switched off the radio and the tape recorder which served as the log.

By now Mitch had returned from the engineering control panel. He looked worried.

"I can't understand it, Jet," he said. "The gauges are right, the fuel tanks are empty. Well, as empty as makes no difference."

"But they can't be. We carried enough reserve for an emergency landing and we haven't used any of that."

"They're dry just the same. What little we have left is in the reserve tanks."

"Impossible. The motor could never burn up fuel at that rate, it would wreck the ship."

Jet was right, of course. But then where had it gone? Less than two hours ago, when the pre-take-off checks were made, the fuel had been there; enough for all our normal needs and some to spare. Now there was virtually none. Should an emergency arise, should we drift off course, or overshoot the landing base, there was nothing we could do about it. These were the thoughts that were flashing through my mind when I made a discovery as startling as that just made by Mitch.

Periodically it was my duty to check and adjust the oxygen supply. I needed no reminder from Jet to carry out this operation. The moment our course for Earth had been set, I had gone over to the air-conditioning panel to carry out my routine. There I found, as Mitch had, that supplies were far less than they should have been. I checked again to make sure. There was no doubt about it. Since taking off from the Moon, one-tenth of our oxygen supply had been used up. I hurried across to Jet to report the news. He ran his fingers through his unruly, black hair and looked at me as though I were crazy.

"What is going on?" he exclaimed. "We couldn't have used up half a day's supply in less than two hours."

"Well, we have," I told him.

Jet was perplexed which wasn't surprising. First the fuel, now the oxygen. The whole thing was fantastic. Impossible. But Mitch's gauges and my indicators did not lie.

After a moment's thought, Jet decided we should search the ship. As he said: "If hundreds of gallons of fuel and half a day's supply of oxygen can disappear in this way other things can disappear, too."

We divided the ship into four parts and every one of us began a thorough check of the portion allotted to him. First we calculated the exact loss of fuel and oxygen. Half an hour later we checked again but found the fuel gauges had remained static and the oxygen was down by only the normal amount needed to replenish the air. All other parts of the ship, batteries, radar, radio and televiewer circuits appeared normal, and in good working order.

At Jet's request, I figured out exactly how long our oxygen supply would last, assuming no further 'evaporation' took place. There was enough for 110 hours, two hours longer than the time required for us to coast back to Earth and make the difficult glide-landing through its atmosphere. We might make it, provided nothing happened to delay us and that we could land without the aid of the motor, which, now that there was insufficient fuel to fire it, was useless anyway.

Our plight was serious; our chances of landing back on Earth safely were slim. We had just about got used to this idea when we received the biggest shock of all.

It came when we examined the food supplies. Luna carried no cook, nor any means whereby food could be heated, for the overall weight of the space craft had had to be kept to the minimum. Liquid, principally cold tea and fruit juice, was drunk from bottles with the aid of straws; solid food was kept in airtight containers and was of the 'snack' variety; bread, cooked meats, cheeses, canned fruit and vegetables. As with the oxygen, we had had sufficient food for thirty-eight days. Thirty-three of those days had already been spent out in space; fourteen days longer than had been intended. Even so there should have been food and drink for another five.

There was. There was, in fact, considerably more; but what, as Lemmy described it, "shook us to the roots" was the fact that the food had completely changed. Instead of tea or fruit juice, the bottles contained only water. And in the solid food containers was a pale yellow, sticky, spongy substance that none of us could recollect ever having seen before. We stared at the stuff incredulously, unable to believe our eyes.

"What on earth has happened to it?" It was Jet speaking. "It seems to have undergone a complete chemical change."

"You once told me," said Lemmy rather bitterly, "that when we reached outer space we would make new and startling discoveries. Well, we have. Fuel evaporates and food turns to something else."

As ship's doctor, the food supplies were my responsibility. Our diet had been carefully planned and the containers, both for the fluids and solids, were of my design. Within them, our precious rations should have kept fresh and wholesome throughout the voyage, even if it had taken longer than we had anticipated – which it had. I could in no way account for this metamorphosis. But, as Lemmy pointed out in his simple but logical way, the important question was not how the food had changed but, since it had, whether it was still good to eat.

There was only one way to find out. I broke off a piece of the strange substance. It was soft and a little sticky, like a newly baked, rich cake. I examined it a moment then placed it, rather gingerly, in my mouth. Taking courage, I crushed it between my teeth and rolled it with my tongue.

"Well, what's it like?" said Mitch. His sun-tanned, leathery face was grim.

"Not bad," I told him. "Rather sweet, like honey, but with the texture of bread. I don't think this will do us any harm."

"It had better not," said Jet. "It's all we've got to live on for the next five days."

"And how about the water?" asked Lemmy.

I took a suck at the straw, held the liquid in my mouth for a few seconds and then swallowed it.

"Clean and fresh," I pronounced. "We'll neither starve nor die of thirst."

"What if there's any delayed action?"

"I don't think there will be, but don't anybody else touch it. If I'm not writhing on the floor within the next three hours we can count it as safe."

"That was a stupid thing to have done, Doc," said Jet. "Supposing it had been poisonous?"

"How else could I have tested it? There's no laboratory aboard this ship and no dog to try the stuff on."

Jet left it at that. He stood in silence while the rest of us waited for him to announce the next move.

"The whole thing beats me," he said at last. "Any of you got any ideas?"

We hadn't. We were all as baffled as he was.

"Well, it couldn't happen for no reason at all, could it?" said Lemmy.

Then Jet thought of my diary. The ship's official log was tape recorded, of course, but, for my own amusement, I had kept a personal diary since before we left Earth. I had continued to keep it throughout the trip and found it a pleasant and satisfying method of passing away the idle hours while we were coasting through space. It also served as a complete record of every man's reaction, including my own, to every circumstance we had met up to now.

And we had been in some very strange circumstances, one way and another, which is why we were now heading back to Earth fourteen days behind schedule. There had been one period when the tape recorder had been out of action for two weeks. During that time my diary became the ship's official log and all that happened to us was recorded by hand as concisely and faithfully as possible.

What prompted Jet to think that my journal might throw light on the mystery I cannot say, but it was bound to have revealed it sooner or later. We merely learned the truth all the quicker; at least, we believe it to be the truth.

Anyhow, at Jet's suggestion. I took the book from my locker, intending to open it at the pages where it had served as the log. But I never got that far. As I flipped the pages something caught my eye that astounded me.

"What is it, Doc?" demanded Jet.

I carefully examined the open page before I made any reply. I just had to be sure that what I saw was really there.

"Today is November 20th, isn't it?"

"Yes, on Earth anyway. What about it?"

"I've made no entry today, not since take-off anyway."

"What's that got to do with anything?"

"A great deal, I think. Here, in my handwriting, is an account of everything we have done since take-off from the Moon, including a fairly comprehensive description of what we saw on the other side."

Jet almost snatched the book out of my hand. He glanced at the entry and turned the leaf over. Then he turned another and another.

He looked up. "There's not only an entry here for today's date," he said, "but for tomorrow's, too, and the next day and the next."

He turned to me angrily. "What is this, Doc – a joke?"

"If it is, it's not me playing it."

"It's your book, isn't it? And this is your handwriting. Who else could have written this stuff?"

"I don't deny that the writing there is mine, or, at least, it's identical with mine, but I swear I have no recollection of writing a word of it."

Jet made no reply. He was reading avidly and, as he did so his expression changed and his ill temper, normally so foreign to Jet, left him. After a few minutes he looked up.

"No, Doc you couldn't have written this," he said slowly. "Not since take-off anyway. You just haven't had the time. And yet the description of the surface of the other side of the Moon is correct in every detail."

"You mean he wrote it before take-off? Before we even saw the other side?" Mitch was putting in his two-cents worth now.

"Yes," said Jet. "That's just what I mean."

"But how the devil could he describe things he had never seen?"

"The same way as he has described the events of tomorrow, and the next day, when they haven't happened yet."

Mitch's mouth fell open. Lemmy gave a grunt of surprise. Heaven knows what I did. I don't remember. Probably just stared wide-eyed at Jet. Of us all, he alone was calm and self-composed.

"Here, gentlemen," he said, "I believe we have the answer. If Doc would be so kind as to read his journal to us, I think it will explain a lot of things. Would you oblige us, Doc?"

I took the book from him. "Where shall I start?"

"With today's entry. After we had encircled the Moon."

I found the place and began to read. It was a weird experience. There before me, in what I could only accept as my own handwriting, the facts were set out, yet I could not recall writing them nor remember any of the events recorded.

"It is now more than two hours since we left the Moon and found ourselves in these new and frightening circumstances..."

The two sentences that followed were enough to show that the circumstances referred to were not those we were experiencing at that moment.

Chapter 2
THE PROJECT

This is my personal account of what happened to the four men who travelled in the first man-made vehicle to reach the Moon. If any other member of the crew were to write a similar account of our adventures, his would probably differ from mine in many ways. But in one respect his would be the same. Of the most momentous happenings neither of us would have any recollection whatever; the only proof (if it is proof) of their occurrence being their inclusion in my journal.

As I write, it is on the cards that we may never reach Earth at all. If we do, landing without the aid of the motor will be difficult and dangerous, and there is every likelihood that we shall crash. The fuel we have in the tanks is not likely to explode (there's hardly enough of it), so much of the equipment, although damaged beyond any further use, should be recoverable. Consequently, unless the ship burns itself out, this narrative will survive the impact and sooner or later the truth will be revealed and accepted or rejected accordingly.

My bet is that it will be the latter. Be that as it may, I will continue to write it during the four and a half days of life we probably have left to us.

If my story is to be complete, I must go back a year or so; before take-off from Earth; before Luna was even built.

The first intimation I had that something big was afoot was when I received a radiogram from my Scots friend Jet Morgan asking me to meet him in, of all places, Adelaide. I'd known Jet for some years, for he often came out to New Mexico where I was employed as director of space medicine at the US high-altitude rocket research grounds at Poker Flats.

In the twenty or so years since the capture of the first German V2, experiments in high altitude rockets had gone on at a spanking pace. In 1957, the first rocket to push its nose up and out of the Earth's atmosphere was launched. By 1960, at colossal expense, another and much more powerful rocket, the A24, a hefty, three-stage affair, had reached free orbit some 750 miles above the Earth's surface. It had been intended to bring it back to base by remote control, but at the crucial moment something went wrong with the missile's intricate inside and it failed to respond. As there was no way of getting a mechanic up there to put the fault right, it remained where it was and, to the best of my knowledge, it's there still.

The launching of the A24 set the world buzzing with excitement. Since World War II there had been constant reports in the press that space travel was just around the corner. The existence of an artificial satellite proved it, or so most people thought. But they hadn't reckoned with a few facts. In the first instance, the placing of a rocket out in space had drained the research department of virtually all its money. In the second, before space travel could become a reality, it was necessary to construct, at the cost of millions upon millions of dollars, a huge space station, also travelling in free orbit, to use as a springboard for the long-distance ships. For, in the light of the knowledge of that time, no rocket could be built that would reach even the Moon in one jump. Moon ships would have to be assembled out in space, and every tiny part of them would first have to be ferried up from Earth to the assembly point. And before the first ship could be constructed, the space station itself had to be put together, and that, too, would have to be ferried out, piece by piece.

The cost would be astronomical – no single government on Earth could afford it. Space travel would, it seemed, have to be left to our descendants, unless, of course, some way could be found to reduce cost. With the type of liquid-fuel rocket then in vogue, there was little hope of that; an entirely new form of propulsion was needed.

But if none of us ever expected to see space travel a reality in our time (and, I may add, least of all me) there was no reason why much of the necessary groundwork to make the dream possible should not be carried out. And that's how I came to be at Poker Flats. As director of space medicine research it was my responsibility, among other things, to design space suits for high-altitude pilots, study the effect of long-period gravityless conditions on the human body (a very difficult task) and the effect of high gravity conditions as well (which was easy).

It was our work at Poker Flats, in conjunction with similar research centres in England, that made superstratosphere passenger flight possible. The principle of the superstratoship is simple. At take-off, it is powered by turbo-jet engines and, under their propulsion, quickly reaches supersonic speed and a height of some 40,000 ft. At that elevation the air is so thin that the turbo-jets cannot function, so they are cut out and liquid fuel rockets take over the job of driving the ship higher and higher into the atmosphere. By the time the rockets are cut out, it is well over the Atlantic, 100 miles high, and travelling at approximately 1,700 mph.

The rest of the journey is unpowered and consists of a gentle glide downwards towards the American coast – rather as a shell, once it has reached maximum height, begins to drop towards its target. The whole trip, from take-off to touch down, takes a little under two hours, enabling passengers to breakfast in London at 7am and reach New York at 4am, in time for another breakfast, if they have a mind for it, three hours after landing. To all intents and purposes, all passengers travelling on the superstratosphere run journey through space, and travel high enough above our atmosphere to see the stars shining in the middle of the afternoon.

Jet Morgan was a pilot on the Atlantic run and three times a week he coaxed his ship to the edge of space. He lived for his work and for his interest in astronautics. Almost every moment of his life was filled with one or the other. He was a leading light of the International Interplanetary Society and flew all over the world to attend their conferences, give lectures or open astronautic exhibitions.

I have lost count of the number of nights Jet and I sat up discussing rockets, space ships and interplanetary travel. I know we must have made, principally for our own amusement, drawings of dozens of ships, satellite stations and fancy rockets of all kinds. Our plans and models were complete to the smallest detail, from space suits, living quarters, air conditioning, food containers and pressure couches to motors, meteor bumper and solar mirror. Moon ships, ferry ships and space station were all systematically dealt with. When it came to designing the radio, televiewer and radar equipment, we were enthusiastically joined by Lemmy Barnet, Jet's first radio operator on the Atlantic run, who, although he did not share our enthusiasm for space travel as such, could never resist the challenge to design some special piece of radio apparatus for any purpose we cared to name. Between the three of us we once constructed a working model of a ship, complete with crew's quarters, that took off, climbed three miles, turned itself over and landed gently on its tail in exactly the way a real ship would have landed on the Moon. The whole operation was radio-controlled.

The hours I spent in the centrifuge and the days I spent watching other guinea pigs undergoing its cruel pressure proved, without a doubt, that it was possible for a man to stand more gravities than he would ever need to experience during a journey to the Moon or planets – should any genius invent a ship economical enough to get him there.

The pressurised suits were, as far as I could tell, quite adequate but, of course, it was impossible to test them under full outer-space conditions. We had a fair idea of how man would react under the long, gravityless periods he would have to spend in space but, for obvious reasons, could never put these theories to a practical test either. So we just continued working and hoped that in the not too distant future our efforts would help launch the first Moon-bound ship on its way. Our hopes were not very high.

Then came the blow. With the first rocket to reach free orbit revolving, uselessly, 700 miles or so above the Earth's surface, all work other than on missiles of a military nature was stopped. I guess Washington considered further research on theoretical space travel to be a waste of time and, further, that, with elections coming up in just a few months, a little widely publicised economy in public funds would not come amiss.

Something like half the personnel at Poker Flats was fired. But space medicine, even when it was for military purposes only, was still an important factor in rocket research so I retained my position although my field was narrowed down so much I was thinking of handing in my resignation.

Then I received the call from Jet whom I had not seen for nearly a month and who had, or so I thought then, no reason whatsoever for being anywhere near Australia. His presence there intrigued me and as the tone of his message was urgent I had little trouble in persuading myself to fly out to Adelaide to see what was going on. I was due for a vacation anyway.

I packed my bags and left New Mexico for New York a week later. I made the journey across the world in two stratospheric hops – New York to Bombay, Bombay to Melbourne – and reached the Australian city the same day. From Melbourne I travelled to Adelaide by aircraft and found Jet waiting to meet me.

He gave me no time to ask questions. I had hardly greeted him when I was swept to another corner of the airfield where a helicopter, its blades already rotating, was waiting. My baggage was bundled inside and I took my seat next to Jet who sat at the controls. Within a few seconds we were in the air, heading over the city towards the irrigated, agricultural land to the north. Five minutes later the pink, sandy wastes of the Australian bush were passing below us.

Jet, in the small pilot's seat, his long legs stretched out before him, seemed taller than ever. His mop of black hair, from which he gained his nickname, was as unruly as ever and there was a glint of good humour in his boyish, grey eyes.

He put the craft on its course, set the automatic pilot, leant leisurely back in his seat and pulled out a pack of cigarettes.

"Well, Doc, how do you like Australia?" he said at last.

"I've hardly had time to form any opinion about it," I told him.

"Not very different from New Mexico, do you think?"

"Not really, but there's a deal more of it."

"How would you like to work in this part of the world?"

"Me? What at?"

"Space medicine research, plus the opportunity to put many of your theories into practice."

"Is there another rocket proving ground out here then besides Woomera?"

"You might call it that. Launching ground would be a better description."

"It amounts to the same thing."

"Not exactly. This is something quite new. It has revolutionized the whole business of rocket construction."

"I don't get you, Jet. Why don't you come to the point?"

"Very well. Within a year from now, a serious attempt will be made to reach the Moon – in one hop."

Had Jet told me he intended to run for President of the United States, I could not have been more surprised. I said nothing for a few moments; instead I gazed at the ground slowly unrolling below us. Ahead was the Flinders Range, a group of hills which, in Australia, pass as mountains. Stretching from below us to the foothills were the sand ridges topped by the inevitable grey-green mulga which is to this sparse country what sagebrush is to the American desert.

"In one hop?" That was all I could say.

Jet laughed. "It's difficult to believe, isn't it, Doc? At first I couldn't myself."

"You do now?"

"Not only that. I'm going. I'm one of the crew."

For the first time I realized he was dead serious. "But to build a rocket that will reach the Moon in one jump is an engineering impossibility. The fuel tanks alone would have to be as tall as skyscrapers."

"With conventional rockets, that's true. But I thought I made it clear, Doc: this is something new – revolutionary."

"It's little short of a miracle."

"It might be at that, but all it comes down to in the end is an atomic motor."

"Atomic?"

"You've heard of Stephen Mitchell?"

"Wasn't he the engineer who designed the first atomic marine motor for the British Navy?"

"Yes. His latest creation is a *rocket* motor."

"How does it work?"

"That I can't tell you, not at the moment. All I can say is that it's small enough and powerful enough to do the job."

I now began to fire enthusiastic questions. Apparently Mitchell's rocket motor, in spite of its compactness, built up sufficient thrust to carry a ship almost to the Moon direct from the Earth's surface. Almost, but not quite. It needed a little assistance.

The free orbit rocket launched from Poker Flats had, as I have said, been a three-stage affair. When it took off from the Earth it was more than 300 feet tall and left its launching platform under the power of its first and largest stage. In less than two minutes its load of more than 5,000 tons of fuel had been burnt and the ship had reached a height of just over 23 miles and was travelling at more than 5,000 mph.

The first stage then dropped away and the second came into action to carry the lightened ship even higher and faster. Two minutes later the 2,000 tons of fuel carried by the second booster had burnt itself out and the ship had reached a height of 40 miles and a speed of nearly 15,000 mph.

Finally the third stage, the smallest of all, carrying the telemetering equipment in its nose, automatically cut in its motor. The second stage, having been discarded, parachuted down to Earth while the ship (now less than a third of its original size) reached a final speed of some 19,000 mph and a height of 750 miles, sufficient to allow it to reach free orbit and enter an ever encircling course round the Earth.

19,000 mph was the highest speed ever reached by a man-made vehicle of any kind, but it was still 6,000 mph less than the speed required to escape entirely from the Earth's gravitational pull.

According to Jet, Mitchell's ship was only of two-stage construction. The first stage worked on exactly the same principle as I have just described but, once its fuel had been used up and the booster had been disconnected, the motor of the second stage, the long-sought, small atomic motor, had the power to increase the speed to more than 27,000 miles an hour, giving the ship sufficient velocity to reach the Moon and a little to spare.

I must have questioned Jet for more than an hour and would have kept up the barrage had he not landed just north of Lake Eyre to refuel. The 'airport' consisted of one small, two-roomed building, an underground fuel storage tank and two mechanics. They ran out to meet us as we taxied in and greeted Jet with a hearty, if coarse, Australian greeting. We climbed out of the cockpit, glad to stretch our legs, and, as stepping outside was rather like stepping into an oven, immediately sought the shade of the white wooden building.

"Make yourself at home," said Jet as he helped himself to a drink from a bottle on the table.

"Is this a private airport?"

"Airport is a fancy name for it, Doc. But we have to refuel somewhere. We're hardly halfway to Luna City yet."

"Luna City?"

"That's what the boys call the launching ground. We have a regular little town there. We're almost completely self-supporting. Fuelling squads come down here on a rota to refill the helicopters that fly between Luna City and Adelaide. When their week is up, they go back to base and their place is taken by somebody else."

We stayed and chatted with the mechanics for a while. Half an hour later we were on our way again and continuing our discussion at the point where landing had compelled us to postpone it.

I finally learned Jet's real reason for inviting me out to Australia. It was to offer me a post, not only as director of the space medicine department of Luna City but also as a member of the crew. He made the offer quite casually some thirty minutes after we had left Lake Eyre and were rapidly approaching the border of Northern Territory and South Australia.

I accepted in the same tone. How I did it so calmly I don't know. I had been offered an active part in one of the greatest and most important experiments in the history of scientific man, and yet all I could say was: "Thank you Jet. I'd like to very much."

"That's fine," Jet replied, and then the talk turned to something else.

I began to understand now that the virtual closing of Poker Flats had more behind it than the mere shortage of money. I also realised why it was that the British had not made any attempt to launch a free-orbit rocket of their own; they had preferred to wait until a more powerful, more economical method of propulsion had been found, and, apparently, they had found it.

Little more than three hours after leaving Adelaide, we reached Luna City. We came upon the site very suddenly for, until we were almost directly overhead, it was hidden from our view. The launching ground was set in the centre of a mountain range high up on the plateau of the Central Desert.

The Horseshoes, as those mountains are called, are part of the Macdonnell Range and are some 250 miles east of Alice Springs.

'Horseshoe' was a perfect description of them; from the air that was just what they looked like. The open end of the shoe faced towards the west. The highest point in the range was exactly opposite the entrance to the enclosed plain and rose about 3,000 feet above it, the plain itself, part of the great, central continental plateau, being some 2,000 feet above sea level. From its highest point the range sloped down on both sides in a curve until, the circle about two-thirds completed, it ran itself into the ground. Inside the shoe the sides of the hills were cliff-like and precipitous, but the outer slopes were fairly gentle.

What struck me at once about this peculiar formation was its similarity to the ringed plains on the Moon. It had the same crumbly, eroded look and, had any telescope-equipped Selenite been able to regard this freakish, terrestrial feature, he would have declared it the one thing on Earth that most nearly resembled his own barren world.

But the most remarkable feature of this semi-enclosed plain was a man-made one: the launching ground. It was, as Jet had said, a miniature city. From above it looked like a giant cartwheel, the hub being the launching platform itself, with the half-completed rocket, enclosed in steel scaffolding, standing on it. The 'spokes' of this giant wheel, which was some four miles in diameter, were roads, every one of which led out from the rocket platform, other minor roads joining the 'spokes' in concentric circles. Arc-shaped buildings filled in the areas outlined by the roads, most of them concentrated towards the outer rim of the wheel.

Jet pointed out a few of the principal blocks to me; living quarters, workshops, centrifuge, cinema, swimming-pool, air strip, sports field hospital, research centre, crew's quarters, stores and so on. Just outside the city, and standing apart from it, was a railroad station from which a single track ran twisting and turning through the low sandhills westwards towards Alice Springs.

"Well, what do you think of her?" asked Jet.

"Why build a launching ground so far away from civilization? This place is outback of the Outback."

"Only place they would give us. If there had been a remoter spot, we'd have got it. They won't run any unnecessary risks. Want to keep us as far away from cities as they possibly can."

We began to descend. As we approached the ground and dropped below the levels of the highest mountain peaks, we lost sight of the great plain beyond. I felt as though I were already landing on another planet. The pinky sand, the red-streaked, precipitous cliffs which, in the clear air, seemed within short walking distance, and the snow-white, man built concrete structures looked for all the world like a Martian landscape with the first Earth colony already established and flourishing.

We touched down. Jet switched off the engine and the rotor blades slowed to a standstill. He slid back the cabin door and we climbed down to the sun-baked ground. A jeep was already on its way out to meet us, hurtling along the concrete road in a cloud of dust. Within a few minutes my baggage had been unloaded from the aircraft and we were speeding across the airstrip towards the crew's living quarters.

Chapter 3
LUNA

"Good morning, gentlemen. The time is 0600 hours. The weather is warm. Temperature at the airstrip is 82 degrees. We can expect it to reach at least 95 degrees by noon."

I awoke with a start, half expecting to see somebody standing in the corner of my room. Instead I saw a panel, some four feet square, placed diagonally across it. At the top was a television screen and underneath three gauze-covered circles marking the positions of intercommunication loudspeakers. Below them were four coloured-glass buttons which, as I was to discover later, were indicator lights. Slowly I realised where I was. I glanced around at the unfamiliar surroundings now flooded with the sunlight which came streaming through the window. The voice was coming from the intercom panel.

"Breakfast will be at 0700 hours as usual. That is all – and thank you."

There was a click and then silence. The phone at my bedside rang. It was Jet.

"Morning, Doc," he said, "have a good night?"

"Very good, thanks, until the talking alarm clock came on."

"Sorry about that. I should have warned you. It happens every day, I'm afraid. See you at breakfast huh?"

I need not fill in every detail of my first week in Luna City. Jet had invited me out there to be director of space medicine and, far more important to me, a member of the ship's crew. But, before being finally accepted, I had to undergo vigorous and, at times, highly unpleasant medical tests. Most of them I had carried out myself on other guinea pigs in the course of my work at Poker Flats.

You cannot send a man up into space, even for a short period, unless he is fighting fit, and the only way to discover whether he can stand up to space flight conditions is to put him through, as far as possible, simulated conditions down on Earth.

It is no exaggeration to say that the series of tests designed for this purpose might well serve to discourage all but the most ardent would-be space traveller. General fitness having been ascertained, the 'patient' is subjected to centrifuge and pressure-chamber tests, both separately and together. He is then called upon to perform certain acts like pressing buttons, repeating memorised passages of prose and arithmetical formulae, and working out fairly complicated problems while under simulated space conditions. If his reactions are good and he does not suffer either physically or mentally from the gruelling tests, he is considered OK.

My tests were spread over the week. I joined the crew at the end of it and our long, concentrated training and preparation for the lunar trip began. And while we were undergoing training, the construction of the rocket went ahead. We and the ship were expected to be ready for each other at approximately the same time.

Rocketship Luna was designed to carry a crew of four; Stephen Mitchell, Jet Morgan, Lemmy Barnet and myself. Lemmy I already knew from the days he had spent with Jet and me when space travel was no more to us than an absorbing hobby and a distant dream. (There have been many occasions over the last few weeks when I am sure Lemmy, at least, wished it had remained so.) Mitch I met at dinner during my first night in Luna City.

I think I would have recognised him as an Australian anywhere. He was tall and slim and looked older than his thirty-six years. He had that casual, nonchalant, patient air, so typical of many Australians, particularly those who have spent most of their lives away from the cities.

Mitch was born in the outback, his father being a cattle rancher and a very successful and prosperous one, too. Steve Mitchell senior had served as flight mechanic in the Second World War and flying was an obsession with him. Small aircraft, including helicopters, were as common on his cattle station, said to be the largest in Queensland, as jeeps were on others.

Young Mitchell had inherited his father's love of everything to do with aircraft and aircraft engines. From the ranch he went to an engineering college in Sydney where he took his degree and afterwards joined the research department of a jet aircraft manufacturer.

He did not remain with them long for he had developed a keen interest in atomic power and was soon offered a remunerative post with the Royal Australian Navy for whom he helped perfect the first atomic motor for use in warships. Three years later a smaller type for submarines was given its trials with most encouraging results.

And then came a big change in Mitch's life. His father died. Mitch put the cattle station into the hands of a manager and took a long vacation to take stock of the future.

He decided he had had enough of ships and felt a strong desire to work in aeronautics again or, better still, astronautics. Astronautics was the new science. The aircraft company for whom he had first worked built many of the research rockets fired at the proving ground at Woomera. Mitch had modified the motors of a number of the liquid-fuel rockets then in use, rendering them more economical in fuel consumption and, in consequence, more efficient in performance.

But liquid-fuel motors had about reached their limit and further development along that line was pointless. It was then that the idea of designing a light atomic motor occurred to him.

The more he thought about it, the more the idea appealed. He resigned his post with the Navy and set to. His drawing office was the converted living-room of his father's ranch house. There he spent long hours of the day and night bent over his board. When he grew tired or felt in need of a mental refresher, he saddled up a horse and rode out on cattle round-ups with the stockmen, living in the open with them for days at a time. At last, some eighteen months later, his plans were complete. He had, he was convinced, found the answer to space travel. Now all he had to do was find an organisation willing – and rich enough – to build the ship to prove it.

But it was soon obvious that no single organisation, private or official, could possibly stand the cost. His only hope lay in persuading a large number of organisations, both governmental and commercial, to share it. He travelled to every corner of the British Commonwealth with a trunkful of plans and a strong line of talk, and succeeded in founding the greatest Commonwealth cooperative effort ever undertaken in peacetime.

Every major aircraft and rocket company contributed towards the cost which, with the building of the rocket and the launching ground, and the personnel to man it, was phenomenal. The Australian Government, beside providing a grant in hard cash, also supplied the site for the launching ground.

The result was Luna City, where every race and tongue of the British Commonwealth of Nations was to be seen and heard. And what a friendly, happy, enthusiastic crowd they were; as an American, I felt it was a great privilege to be a principal member of this team.

Sitting at the same dinner table as Mitch, and hearing him speak in his broad Australian accent, I found it hard to convince myself that he was the man primarily responsible for it all. His manner was a bit rough, his jokes apt to be somewhat coarse and his conversation blunt and straight to the point. He expected others to speak their minds, too.

"As soon as we've had dinner," he said, when we had about finished anyway, "we'll hop in a truck and show you round the place."

"Perhaps Doc would like to go to bed," suggested Jet. "He's just flown halfway across the world. He must be tired."

"He doesn't look tired." Mitch looked at me with cold, unblinking eyes. "Are you tired, Doc?"

"No – not really. I'd like to take a look at a few things before it gets dark."

"Good. Not that there's all that much to see yet. Half the buildings are unfinished and outside the City there's nothing but the Never-Never. You never saw such a godforsaken place."

As the weeks went by, the building of Luna and Luna City progressed steadily. The city was finished first – by an army of builders working day and night. Control room, deep shelters, radio transmitter, radar stations, film unit, deep fuel storage tanks and a host of other buildings were erected and the technical equipment installed.

During these early months, we paid little attention to the activity going on all around us; we were too preoccupied with our own affairs. Our training began with intensified lectures on astronomy and astronavigation. We spent hours in the observatory stargazing and studying lunar geography. Hundreds of photographs of Sinus Iridum, where it was intended we should land, were studied until we knew the area by heart. In addition, there was a vast relief map of the Bay for our use, showing every known crater, crevice, depression and mountain.

Take-off and landing procedures were gone over time and again. And during the toughening up processes we spent hours in the centrifuge and the pressure chambers. We also received training in mountain climbing and laboured up and down the precipitous walls of the Horseshoes, both with and without space suits, until Lemmy remarked that anyone might think we were a mountaineering expedition.

Every man's individual training was, of course, primarily concerned with his own specialised work as a crew member, but he also had to learn a great deal about every other man's job so that, in the event of one of us falling sick or being otherwise incapacitated, another would be able to step into his place.

Jet was captain, pilot, chief navigator and second engineer. Mitch was chief engineer, second pilot and navigator. Lemmy was radio, radar and televiewer operator and chief electronic engineer. I was ship's doctor and responsible for the efficient working of oxygen supply air-conditioning, and food. I was also principal photographer. If the necessity arose, I could take over most of Lemmy's duties and he mine.

In addition to being trained to man the ship, we received instructions as to how to carry out some elementary scientific research and exploration during the fourteen days we would spend on the Earth's satellite. Our work would consist, principally, of photographing the heavens, particularly the sun and planets, selecting small specimens of moon rock and soil to bring back to Earth, measuring the radioactivity of parts of the Moon's surface within the landing area and studying the formation and composition of craters within easy reach.

The building of the rocket was a slow process but, gradually, enclosed in the splints of the erection gantry, it began to climb towards the sky. The first stage, the booster, was finished within three months and by the end of six months the second stage was well on the way to completion, the atomic motor being installed and the crew's cabin wired up.

I watched its progress every night. The crew's quarters were set apart from the rest and were cool, soundproof and comfortable. The four rooms, one for each crew member, were housed in a building that contained the ablutions, rest room, games room and dining room. Each bedroom was approximately twenty feet square and contained a bed, a bedside table, writing desk, bookcase and wardrobe and the intercommunication panel I have already described.

The television screen served three purposes. With the correct combination of buttons situated in the control board just above the bed, it was possible to select either a television programme relayed from Adelaide, the film being shown in the camp cinema or a view of the rocket, long shot or close-up, under construction. Always, before I finally put out the light and went to sleep, I looked in on the rocket for a few minutes to see how she was coming on. I shall not easily forget the sight of her, standing there, brilliantly illuminated by the arc lamps and surrounded by dozens of supply trucks. Up and down the gantry shot elevators carrying construction engineers and prefabricated parts of the ship. Directly behind her were the tallest peaks of the Horseshoe range with the observatory nestled comfortably on the top. The observatory was the last object to reflect the rays of the setting sun at night and the first in the morning when, with the sun behind it, it stood out against the jagged skyline in silhouette.

The ship was almost complete now, complete enough for us to occupy the cabin and go through the take-off routine. For nearly a week we lived in her, going through every procedure of take-off, flight and landing on the Moon. We lived under identical conditions of space flight, except that we were earthbound. Our air supply was oxygenized, our food taken cold. When we stepped out of the ship, it was through an airlock and in space suits. We unloaded the astronomical gear, cameras and geiger counter and solemnly set about exploring the Horseshoe plain as though we were already on the Moon. We chipped out samples of rock, collected and boxed handfuls of dust and radioed our findings back to base – less than ten miles away.

At last we were ready. On the day before take-off we worked up to the last moment, had dinner at seven and retired to bed. We had been told to relax and sleep.

It was easier said than done. It had been a hot day – an extremely hot day. Official reading down at the air strip had reached 112°F in the shade. Over at the launching platform the ground crew, most of them naked from the waist up except for that peculiarly national piece of Australian headwear, the bush hat, had labored in the merciless sun from dawn to dusk, working against time to have everything checked, rechecked and ready for the fuel crews to take over. As the sun went down, the last of them put on his shirt, climbed aboard the passenger truck and went hurtling across the desert towards the living quarters, a cool shower and a lusty supper in the ground staff canteen.

As the platform crew trucks arrived, those of the fuel crews left, the men aboard them donning their protective clothing as they went. An hour later the pump lines had been connected and the transfer of hundreds of tons of highly explosive liquid fuel and oxydiser from their underground storage to the ship's tanks had begun.

I watched the fuellers at work on the screen. I had drawn the curtains of the window and rays of light from an eight-day old Moon entered the opening at an angle, illuminating the notebooks and text books piled up on the table.

Outside, as darkness fell, I knew that the cries of the dingos would mingle with the low, powerful hum of the pump motors. I imagined the orders barked at the men as they climbed the gantries, disconnected and reconnected the lines and kept a watchful eye on the gauges. Every man, completely enclosed in his suit, received his orders via his personal radio and made his reports back to Control in the same way. Fuelling was a tough, skilful and dangerous job and it was carried out to a precise routine. They would be at it for hours yet, almost until take-off time.

I lay on my back, trying to compose my thoughts sufficiently to allow me to sleep. I had partially succeeded when I was jerked awake by the sound of low voices. Over in the corner, two of the indicator lights glowed on the intercommunication panel.

By means of the intercom we, the four members of the crew, could talk to one another. If we wished, we could all converse at the same time. We could, of course, eavesdrop as well. Normally we never did. If any one of us was expected to take part in a discussion, his own coloured indicator light would show. My own light was not flicking but Jet's amber and Lemmy's green were.

I realised I must have forgotten to switch off my receiver after we had all wished each other good night. I started to get out of bed. But then I stopped myself. It might have been my own thoughts that were being spoken out loud by the two familiar but disembodied voices.

"Were you asleep, Jet?"

"Does it sound like it?"

"I can't sleep either." Lemmy sounded lonely and just a little anxious. "I can't believe it, Jet. It's all a dream, isn't it? Tomorrow we'll wake up and find ourselves back on the superstrato run, won't we?"

"I hope not, Lemmy. I'd hate to have gone through the last nine months' training for nothing."

"That's what worries me. That it might be for nothing."

"I don't understand you."

"Suppose something goes wrong."

"Why should it?"

"Something could have been forgotten. Some miscalculation made."

"The chances are remote. Everything has been checked and rechecked, both by human and electronic brains."

"But it could happen. There's always a chance."

"About as much chance as you have of winning the football pools."

"I won fifty pounds not two months back."

"I mean the big prize – thousands of pounds."

"I've got a feeling, Jet. Nobody's ever made this run before. Anything could happen."

"Not to the ship."

"To us then."

"You've got the jitters, Lemmy. We all have. It's only natural. Think back to the first superstrato crossing we made. We felt much the same way then, remember?"

"This is different, Jet. You'd think that at least they'd have sent an unmanned rocket first."

"You couldn't bring it back, so what would be the point?"

"Well, at least they'd know it could get there, that would be something."

"Luna will get there – and back, too. Little more than three weeks from now, Lemmy, you'll be laughing at yourself for talking this way."

"I'm not laughing now."

"Try to sleep. Tomorrow you'll be OK."

"I told you – I *can't* sleep. Have you looked at the ship lately?"

"I switched on the screen just before I got into bed. Why?"

"They're still pumping the juice into her."

"They'll be doing that for an hour or two yet. You'd do better to switch your viewer off and try to forget about it."

"I've tried, but it's all I think of."

"Then take your pill. In ten minutes you'll be sound asleep."

"Why don't you take yours?"

"That's just what I intend to do – now."

"Oh. You sure you wouldn't like to talk a few minutes longer?"

"No thanks, Lemmy."

"All right. Good night."

"Good night."

"Jet –"

"Oh, go to sleep."

There was a sharp click and the amber light went out.

I settled back between the sheets, reached out for my own pill, swallowed it and waited for sleep to overtake me.

Chapter 4
TAKE-OFF
FROM EARTH

It was still dark when I awoke. I looked at my watch. Half past four. I switched on the televiewer and a blurred image of the ship's gantry appeared on the screen. It sharpened as the instrument warmed up and showed the launching platform to be deserted but for the guards. There was no sign of a fuelling truck or any other vehicle.

I lay and watched the bored perambulations of the sentries for nearly half an hour before I switched the televiewer off again and thought about getting up. We were due to be called at 5am. At that time, precisely, the intercom speaker clicked on and the usual official, precise voice greeted me with a commentary on the weather and the expected rise in temperature at noon. I wondered why. It was no concern of ours. We would not be here to feel it. Heaven knows what we would be feeling at noon, Luna City time, away out there thousands of miles above the surface of the turning globe where time stood still and noon was always with us.

Perhaps I had mistaken the day. Maybe this was not Z day after all but just another in the long training schedule. But the voice soon put me right.

"Take-off time is zero minus two hours," it announced. "Breakfast will be served early, at 0530 hours. Crew suits will be worn and all personnel will assemble in the briefing room at 0600 hours precisely. That is all, gentlemen. Thank you – and good luck."

The last three words were said with a warmth that was completely alien to the voice as I had known it during the last nine months.

I shaved, zipped on my crew suit and made my way to the dining room to find the other three already there. Breakfast, the last hot meal we expected to have for nearly a month, was eaten in an air of forced cheerfulness and good humour.

Afterwards we assembled in the briefing room for our final instructions, said goodbye to chiefs of various departments and, with handshakes all round, made our way to the crew jeep which was waiting outside.

The door opened to a ring of cheers, for every worker not engaged in take-off routine was out there to see us off. They swarmed round the jeep as we got into it. The roar we got as we moved off towards the launching platform must have been heard at Alice Springs.

Lemmy, who had been a little subdued and less talkative than the rest of us, brightened up considerably during this spontaneous demonstration and wore a beaming smile as he turned in his seat to wave goodbye. As we sped towards the launching site the crowd broke up and the men who had composed it began to race towards the main underground shelter to race for the best seats in front of the televiewer.

We reached the launching platform within five minutes. The control room director was waiting for us. He accompanied us up the steps of the launching apron as far as the elevator which was enclosed within the labyrinth of steel scaffolding. The elevator was merely a platform. It had no sides and no roof.

As we began to ascend, the controller yelled his goodbyes and good lucks at us and we yelled and waved back. Three faint cheers came up to us from the guards who had formed a tight little group down on the ground and were waving their bush hats to punctuate the timing of their cheers.

"Goodbye, Earth," said Lemmy. "I've set foot on you for the last time."

"Not the last time," said Jet.

"It feels like the last time."

The walls of steel rods went flashing past. About half a mile to the south three rockets soared into the air and burst into a shower of red sparks which fell to the ground like a great meteoric display. It was the first signal; the first warning that take-off was near and that the launching area must now be cleared.

The elevator jolted to a stop. The entrance to the air lock stood open, its door folded back into the ship. We could see Luna City spread out below us, see the lights of the jeep which had brought us receding into the darkness as it carried the guards towards the viewing shelters. The controller's car made its way to the control room and disappeared into the underground park.

We were now alone. Utterly alone. The only men in the area with their heads above ground.

"All right, we don't need to stand here admiring the view," said Jet. "Let's get inside."

We clumped our way across the wooden platform, through the circular opening and onto the steel floor of the airlock. There was just about enough room to accommodate the four of us. We paused as Jet, leading the way, climbed the ladder that led through another circular hole in the ceiling and into the cabin.

I went next. The rungs of the ladder felt cold to my hands which, I must confess, were sweating a little at the palms. Once through I turned to give a hand to Lemmy who was following me.

"Here we are," he said as his head popped out of the hole.

"Home, sweet home."

I heaved him out of the opening and then gave my hand to Mitch.

We were now under Jet's orders. He wasted no time.

"Lemmy," he said, "open up the radio. Carry out pre-take-off checks."

"Yes, Jet." Lemmy moved over to the control table.

"Carry out your checks, Doc, and you, Mitch."

We set to. Base was contacted, televiewers, radar, fuel gauges and oxygen supply checked. Suddenly a siren sounded, its wail coming up through the air lock like a voice from another world.

"Second warning," said Lemmy unnecessarily.

The wailing faded away just as the check routine was completed. We reported our findings to Jet who logged "Check OK" on the tape recorder. Then he turned to the three of us and said:

"It will be half an hour before they remove the gantry and are ready for firing. We'll all lie down while we're waiting. Relax. Don't talk unless you have to. Radio will be left on. Ignore it if you can."

I stretched out on my bunk which was underneath Jet's. We had gone through this routine often, the last three times within the ship. Take-off procedure had been rehearsed in every detail, the only difference between then and now being that we had not left the ground. Jet's orders had always been couched in exactly the same words. Even so they sounded fresh, had a different tone about them. The very cabin looked different. The atmosphere was different This was real; before it had seemed play.

For the first time I noticed how small the cabin was. I could, by reaching up, almost touch the underside of Jet's bunk and my own was less than two feet from the floor. The other two bunks – their official designation was 'take-off couches' – were only ten feet away. They were of exactly the same design as mine and Jet's, of course, and were occupied by Mitch below and Lemmy above. Short ladders led to the upper bunks.

The shiny-new cabin was spherical, its flat floor being set low in the sphere. Consequently the walls and ceiling, except where control boards had been built against them, were dome shaped. In the centre of the ceiling was a circular hatch. This was the entrance to the pilot's cabin, used only during the landing period of the return journey to Earth for, although the ship took off vertically, it landed horizontally like a superstratocruiser. For such flights our bunks could be converted into chairs. The cabin then became lopsided like a living room that had been tipped over to allow one of its walls to become the floor and the opposite one the ceiling. But this was unimportant for, by the time this tipping-up process was necessary, our journey would be virtually over and there would be nothing to do but sit tight until the landing had been made.

Below the cabin floor was the airlock and the emergency access hatch to the fuel tank area. Running from below the cabin floor and deep down into the motor was a long, narrow tube which carried the connecting wires from the control boards. Almost immediately it ran through a specially treated, thick sheet of circular lead which served to separate us from the radioactivity set up by the motor. Below the protective sheet were the spherical fuel tanks; below them the motor itself. The fuel tanks and motor combined filled a greater area of space than the rest of the second stage put together.

The pilot's cabin, the crew's cabin, the fuel tanks and all but the exhaust of the motor were enclosed in a conventional, rocket-shaped shell which, as protection against the unlikely possibility of a meteoric collision, was again enclosed in an outer wall of identical shape, an inch or more of space being left between the two hulls.

We could hear the voice of Control calling the out-stations to report. One by one they checked in; radar, televiewer, observatory, firing control, radio transmitter. Personnel deep shelter reported 'all under cover'. And through it all, the automatic speaking clock:

" *Zero, minus 20 minutes.*"

Jet announced the next orders. "Fasten safety straps."

We pulled them into position and made them fast.

"Position control panels."

There was a faint hum as the four panels slid out from the wall into their take-off positions a foot above our faces. Each panel contained the gauges applicable to the duties of each crew member. Mine contained the oxygen, air conditioning and temperature indicators. I also controlled the flywheel stabilisers. Jet's indicator would tell him full details of line of flight, speed and acceleration during take-off. Mitch would watch the performance of the motors while Lemmy had the radio, radar and televiewer controls duplicated on his panel. In one respect the panels were identical. They all carried a small televiewer screen and intercom microphone.

"Hullo, Luna. May we remove the elevator?"

Only Jet answered Control during take-off. "Go ahead."

"*Zero, minus 19 minutes.*"

"Lemmy, televiewer – control view."

"Control view one."

The screens came to life and showed an image of the ship as seen by the control room. It was relayed up to us via the teletransmitter. The rocket was still enclosed within the gantry and looked very tiny, like a model. It was difficult to believe that I was actually within the ship.

"Stand by Luna. Airlock and outer door closing."

There was a click of relays and a whirr. The circular airtight door which was to seal off our tiny cabin sank slowly into the floor, then the deeper hum of the automatic outer door control filled the ship. A click, a clump, and then silence, followed almost immediately by a hiss of air that quickly faded away.

"Airlock closed."

"*Zero, minus 18 minutes.*"

We were completely cut off from the outside world now. Automatically the oxygen supply came on. The dials on my panel showed the pressure.

"Oxygen, Doc?"

"OK."

The seconds ticked by.

"*Zero, minus 15 minutes.*"

Jet ran over take-off routine for the last time and ended:
"Remember, everything has been checked and rechecked. Nothing can go wrong."

The addition was not in the book. Mitch raised his eyebrows enquiringly and looked up towards Jet's bunk.

"Keep your ears open for Control. They may need to send new instructions once we're under way, but we probably won't be able to do anything about them until acceleration ceases."

"Zero, minus 10 minutes."

"They're moving the gantry." It was Lemmy who spoke. I looked at the screen. The scaffolding, all in one piece, was backing away from the ship. Within a couple of minutes it had moved into the background of the picture, leaving the rocket bare. It was the first time any of us had seen her out of the splints. She looked magnificent, even in the small frame. I glanced at the large televiewer screen over the main control panel to get a better view.

Although her base was more than ninety feet in diameter, her height and the way she tapered off to the fine point of the antenna in her nose gave her a slim, graceful appearance like a gigantic obelisk. She was nearly twice as high as Nelson's column and her whole weight seemed to rest on the tips of the four great stabilizer fins. In fact they barely touched the ground. It was the rim of the exhaust of the huge, liquid fuel motor of the booster stage that carried the ship's weight as she stood poised over the deep exhaust tunnel on the flanges of curved, steel supports. But, due to the bowl-shaped launching area, so designed to reduce the danger from an accidental explosion, the supports could not be seen. It was impossible to tell that the ship was built in two stages. Just above where the separation line might have been visible were the two great swept-back ailerons and, near the nose, were the smaller ones, sloping back to the same angle. Just below them, like an elongated blister, was the pilot's canopy.

The first streaks of dawn began to light up the sky. Until a moment ago the floodlit rocket had stood out against a black background, but it was now possible to detect the silhouetted, jagged outline of the hills behind it.

"*Zero, minus 5 minutes.*"

We waited in silence.

"*Four minutes.*"

Jet gave his final warning before firing time. "When we're under way, lie flat. During the first acceleration period we will reach nine g's."

"Hope somebody remembered to buy return tickets for this trip." Lemmy reacted to his own joke but there was no response from anyone else.

"*Three minutes.*"

Jet's tense voice broke in on Lemmy's. "Doc, gyro."

"Gyro," I repeated, and pressed the contact. I could feel the hum of the flywheel through the steel supports of my bunk.

"*Two minutes.*"

"*One.*"

Down in the concrete, sunken blockhouse that was the control room, six rows of ten indicator lights were illuminated on the firing panel. As each second passed one light went out.

"Stand by for firing."

"Recorder, Lemmy."

"Recorder on."

"*Zero, minus 30 seconds.*"

"Lemmy, lie still!"

"Only getting comfy."

A red button of light was flashing on Jet's panel. Once every second.

"*Twenty seconds.*"

Down in the control block a button was pressed and the ignition circuit completed. A wisp of white vapour drifted up from the base of the rocket.

"*19, 18, 17, 16, 15...*"

The wisp of smoke became a belch of flame. The fuel pumps came to life, slowly at first and then at full force as consumption increased to an almost insatiable level. The tongue of flame shot down into the jet deflector. There it turned the cooling waters into steam which was propelled along the tunnel shaft, under the apron and up and out of the safety vent a hundred yards from the rocket like a powerful, natural geyser.

"*14, 13, 12, 11 . . .*"

The noise, even to us in the ship, was almost unbearable. It began to drown out the speaking clock.

At ten seconds a row of ten white lights, the first of which was situated immediately below the flashing one, came on. Jet, thinking we might not hear the voice of Control, took his time from the lights and yelled off the seconds as each one went out.

"*10, 9, 8, 7, 6 . . .*"

My mouth went dry. I shot a glance over towards Mitch. He was lying quite still, his eyes fixed on the indicators of his panel. I turned back to the small picture of the rocket on the screen before my face.

"*5, 4, 3, 2, 1 – fire!*"

I felt the ship stir; give a very slight roll. She was leaving the ground. Slowly, slowly, one foot, two feet, three feet, four.

"*Plus 1 second.*"

The gap between the platform and the base of the first stage was quite appreciable. The ship seemed to be balanced, perfectly balanced, on the bright flame of its exhaust. We were nine feet off the ground.

"*Plus 8 seconds.*"

Height, a thousand feet. The picture on the screen was still that as seen from below. As it rose higher, the rocket got smaller, a column of fire and smoke trailing behind it.

"Lemmy, televiewer – rear view."

"Televiewer, rear view – on."

The picture changed. The view was now directly below us. A bird's-eye view of Luna City.

"*Twenty seconds.*"

Height, 6.8 miles. Now we could see the whole Horseshoe Range and a great deal of the country around it.

Velocity, 4,000 mph. The pressure began to tell. I could not move a limb, not a muscle. It was as though I was made of lead. Lemmy began to groan.

"Thirty seconds."

Height, 27.2 miles. Velocity, 6,550 mph. A great weight had settled on my chest. I found it difficult to breathe. Lemmy was screaming, whether with pain or with fear I had no means of knowing.

A few moments later we soared into the sunlight. It came streaming through the deeply-tinted, thick glass that was our only porthole, a brilliant spotlight on the cabin wall. We learned later from Control that the observatory staff, following our course with the telescope, saw us shoot into the sunlight. One moment we were invisible – all but the flaming exhaust – the next we were illuminated, lit up by the sun.

"Eighty seconds."

Height, 76 miles. Velocity 11,000 mph.

The pain in my limbs and chest was excruciating. I could not help but cry out. Then the acceleration stopped with nauseating suddenness; the motor of the first stage had burnt itself out.

Lemmy and I stopped yelling and silence fell upon the cabin. In the televiewer I could see the Earth – the pink earth of Australia with the dawn creeping across its surface; an ill-defined line that separated light from darkness. Luna City, now only a tiny spot set in what seemed to be a perfectly shaped horseshoe, lay in the half light.

"Tanks empty, booster paid out," called Mitch. He sounded a little weary.

"Stand by to jettison booster," replied Jet.

"Standing by."

"Contact!"

There was a sharp muffled explosion as the huge booster was disconnected. Immediately the screen was blacked out by a closeup view of the useless stage as it began to fall behind. It receded slowly for, although the jettison action had slowed it down and speeded us up very slightly, it was of course still climbing at almost the same rate as ourselves. Then the steel mesh parachute automatically opened. Even in the thin air of the upper atmosphere in which we were now travelling, the parachute had a fairly powerful braking effect and the image of the empty, blunt-nosed hulk began to diminish rapidly.

The time to cut in the atomic motor and gain our final burst of speed was almost on us. Jet was already calling base.

"Hullo, Control. Booster jettisoned. Standing by to cut in second motor. Awaiting your signal. Over."

The seconds ticked by in silent expectation as I waited for Control to give the OK, but no sound came from my earpiece. Jet repeated his call. There was still no answer.

"My head-set is out of action," he said. "Any of you get their reply?"

None of us had.

"Lemmy, any idea what might be wrong?"

"Receiver and transmitter working satisfactorily according to the indicators. I'll try the g.p. speaker."

That was dead too.

"Maybe the amplifying circuit's packed in," went on Lemmy. "Wouldn't surprise me if the shock of the jettison smashed every valve in the ship."

"We can't wait much longer, Jet." Mitch was impatient. "We're losing momentum every second. Unless we take full advantage of our present speed we'll never make it."

"I'll give them one more try. Unless they answer immediately, we'll use our own judgment and fire the motor manually. Hullo, Control – Luna calling. Come in please."

Silence. The booster was still behind us, gradually getting smaller, a black disc against the background of the glaring, pink Earth.

"Stand by, Mitch, we'll give her a full burst. Whole of tank one."

"Check."

"Everybody battened down? The acceleration will be high. Things will be tough for a bit."

"Oh no," groaned Lemmy.

"OK, Mitch?"

"OK."

"Fire!"

There was a sound like the roar of a thousand heavy guns, a passing express train, a colossal waterfall and a clap of thunder. The ship trembled like a leaf, steadied herself and began at once to increase her velocity. We were no longer rising vertically but at an angle to our original line of flight, entering the set course which, if all went well, would carry us towards the exact spot where the Moon would be in less than five days from now.

If the pressure experienced during the first firing period had been unpleasant, this was ten times worse. All the sensations of heaviness and the great weight on the chest came quicker than before. I felt as though I were being pushed through the couch. The muscles of my thighs seemed to flatten outwards. The loose flesh on my face pressed down on to my cheek bones. It was as though a pair of powerful hands had been placed on each cheek and were trying to pull the flesh from my face towards my ears. My mouth stretched until it hurt. My tongue was too heavy to lift and saliva gathered in the back of my throat. Breathing was well nigh impossible. I began to yell, to moan and scream. It was the only way I could force the breath out of my lungs. They seemed to fill of their own accord causing me to sing out in deep, sucking, involuntary sobs. Had I been able to do so, I would have kicked my legs, waved my arms in the struggle to breathe. I expected my lungs to collapse.

The agony lasted for a full two minutes. Then it ceased. The suddenness with which the motor cut out and the deep silence that followed set bells ringing in my ears. Mitch passed the back of his hand across his forehead. His face was ash coloured.

Gradually the ringing faded away and my hearing returned. I heard Lemmy speak – as from a distance.

"Is it over?"

"Yes, Lemmy. Feel OK?"

"Like I've been through a mangle."

"Doc?"

"OK, I think."

"Mitch?"

Mitch didn't answer – not at first. He attempted to say something but was unable to speak. He was trying hard not to vomit. So was I.

"What's up, Mitch?"

"I – feel – like – death." He got the words out only with great effort.

"Lie still. Don't move. We'll all lie still for a few minutes."

Presently I began to feel better. So did Lemmy. In fact he was almost objectionably cheerful.

"Lemmy, if you feel fit enough, get up and get to work on that radio. We must re-establish contact with base as soon as possible."

"Oh sure, Jet. Leave it to me." He undid his safety straps, sat up in his bunk, took off and went drifting up to the ceiling. I've never seen such a look of horror and surprise on a man's face as I did at that moment. Lemmy lay against the cabin roof, face down, his arms and legs spread out awkwardly.

"Jet – get me down. Help!"

"Serves you right for getting off your bed without your boots on. You should know better than that."

"All I did was reach out for them and I shot straight up here."

"You should have held on to your couch. The slightest movement is likely to send you drifting. It's been drummed into you often enough."

"Pull yourself down by the rail, Lemmy," I called.

He did as I suggested. "Oh," he said, "I feel just like a feather."

None of us weighed as much. We were all weightless, as was everything in the ship, and would remain so until we landed.

"Is it going to be like this all the way to the Moon, Doc?"

"I'm afraid so, Lemmy. But you'll get used to it. Now, gently – not too hard – you'll hit the floor."

He reached his bunk without incident and, hanging on to the side with one hand, pulled his boots from their stowage locker with the other. He secured himself with his safety strap and put on his metal-soled, magnetic boots. He was then ready to descend to the floor, which he did, negotiating the rungs of the ladder rather drunkenly. But once he touched the floor he was able to stand up and, with the clumsy steps of a robot, stagger across the cabin.

"What's it like to walk, Lemmy?" I asked. I was feeling much better now and was putting on my own boots as I spoke.

"Like your feet are anchored but your head's adrift."

I stepped out of my bunk and stumbled across to Lemmy. It was a weird sensation, but after a few practice trips round the cabin Lemmy and I were walking almost normally. But there were a few things that took some getting used to. For example, if you held up your arm it had a tendency to stay up. It needed as much muscular power to get it down again as it needed to raise it. It would not drop back to a hanging position as it would on Earth.

"Try walking up the wall," suggested Jet good humouredly.

"Huh?"

"Yes, come on, Doc," said Lemmy. "You go one way, I'll go the other. I'll meet you by the pilot's hatchway in the roof."

Climbing up the wall was no more difficult than walking across the floor. I had picked a path free from control boards and ascended with ease. The cabin seemed to half turn over as I climbed. When I reached the ceiling it was to see Lemmy advancing towards me with a wide grin.

"Doctor Matthews, I presume. Allow me to introduce myself. Lemmy Barnet, the human fly."

We both grinned. We couldn't help it. It was such a fantastic, enjoyable situation.

Oddly enough, although Lemmy and I were standing on the ceiling, we had absolutely no sensation of being upside down. But the cabin looked haywire. The ceiling was our floor, the floor the roof, and it was Jet on his bunk and Mitch lying on his who appeared to be the wrong way up. It was hard to believe that they would not come crashing down on us at any moment.

"Don't hang about up there like that," said Mitch suddenly. "I feel bad enough as it is. And what about that radio?"

"Yes, come on, Lemmy," laughed Jet. "Cut out the fun and games – we've got work to do."

Mitch's stern comments brought us all back to our senses. We recrossed the ceiling and came 'down' the walls again to floor level. I carried out my routine check of the control board under my care and, while Jet carried out his inspection for him, I went over to talk to Mitch.

"How are you feeling?"

"Crook, Doc, very crook."

"Well, the radar's still working anyway." Lemmy, over by the main control table, was talking to no one in particular.

Mitch was suffering from a bad attack of space sickness. He was the oldest member of the crew and it was no more than I expected. I told him to rest for a couple of hours, then he would feel more himself again. But Mitch had no intention of resting; in fact he became very argumentative.

"How long is it going to take Lemmy to put that radio right?" he demanded.

"Give him a chance," Jet replied. "He's hardly started work on it yet."

"And what if he doesn't put it right?"

"Why shouldn't he? He knows every valve, screw and condenser in the ship. Whatever the fault is, he'll find it."

"I wish I could think so. How do we know our height, speed or anything else unless we can contact base?"

"If it comes to it we can take some fixes on the sun and the planets."

"Then I'd better get over to the astrodome and start." He raised himself up in his bunk. Jet pushed him flat again.

"Oh no, Mitch. You stay where you are until Doc says you're in a fit condition to get up. Now take it easy. In a few minutes Lemmy will be through to Control and everything will be all right. Give him a pill, Doc."

As Jet turned away from Mitch to go over to where Lemmy was tinkering with the radio he gave me an enquiring raise of his eyebrows. Mitch had a little trouble swallowing his pills, but twenty minutes later he was asleep.

"When he wakes again," I thought to myself, "he'll find contact with base has been re-established and he'll have a sweeter temper."

I couldn't have been more wrong – about the contact, or Mitch.

Chapter 5
ACTION STATIONS!

Many hours had passed. Mitch and I were trying to get some rest while Jet worked with Lemmy. It wasn't easy to sleep, but we lay on our bunks, so far as it is possible to lie down under gravityless conditions, and did our best. But after only a few minutes, Mitch called over to the two men at the control table and said:

"How's it going?"

Jet came over to us so that Lemmy wouldn't hear his reply.

"He's still got half the radio equipment all over the table," he said quietly.

"Isn't he ever going to find the trouble? Two days he's been at it now – and not a peep out of the darned radio."

"Now take it easy, Mitch. He's doing his best. He's been working all this time with no sleep. He can't do more than that."

Mitch turned pale. His lips compressed and I noticed he was clenching his fists. "We should never have brought him."

Only the slight edge of Jet's voice betrayed that he was having difficulty in keeping his own feelings under control.

Mitch was beginning to shout now. "Why does he have to take so darned long? Doesn't he know that every second is carrying us further away from the Earth – probably to our deaths?"

This was, of course, true – in part, at any rate. All this time, although the rocket was constantly losing velocity, we were coasting further and further from Earth and closer to the Moon. And for the last few hours, apart from our routine checks, there had been little any of us could do except be patient and hope that Lemmy would be able to put the radio right. I glanced over at his stocky form bent over the radio panel. He worked in silence now. He had been bright enough when he started but, as the tension in the cabin grew, Lemmy become more and more reticent, working with grim desperation. I realised that he considered the failure of the radio to be his personal responsibility. He had, of course, supervised the designing of the equipment and helped install it but, although he had been working on it incessantly, he could find no fault with it.

Fortunately the radar and televiewers were still functioning satisfactorily, and every hour or so we turned on the viewer to look at the Earth, now no more than a large globe on the screen; a globe that was ever decreasing in size. When we took our first look, only two hours after take-off, the whole Australian continent filled the screen. But gradually, as we rose higher, it decreased in size and a greater area of the Earth came into view. Soon we could identify almost the whole of Asia and, six hours later as the globe turned on its axis, Africa was spread out before us.

On the land masses not obscured by cloud we could quite easily make out the mountains, the forest areas, the deserts and even the larger rivers. But by the time the American continent had swung into view this was no longer possible and, except where the sun was rising over the high mountain ranges, causing them to throw long shadows across the plains, the Earth looked flat.

Now, some twenty hours after take-off, the vast expanse of the Pacific Ocean filled the screen, the tiny islands with which it is studded looking like defects on the surface of a vast sheet of bright-blue glass.

As part of the globe was always in darkness it resembled a great moon at first quarter. Every time we took a fresh look at the retreating Earth, we could measure the distance it had rotated on its axis; fifteen degrees every hour. At first it had been fascinating to watch the countries of the hemisphere facing us pass from darkness into light and then disappear round the eastern limb of the globe. We pointed out to one another the large cities such as Johannesburg, New York, San Francisco and Los Angeles, but as the hours dragged by the game palled. Other thoughts intruded, like the ones Mitch was voicing now.

"Doesn't Lemmy realise that without the radio we're flying blind?

"Oh, it's not that bad, Mitch," Jet's calm voice replied. "We can figure out our approximate speed and position if it comes to it. Let's give Lemmy a couple of hours more."

I felt much reassured by this news, but Mitch apparently did not.

"A couple of hours! If you ask me, he'll never get that radio going. What happens if he doesn't get through to Control at all?"

"We'll wait a couple of days until our velocity has dropped to its minimum and then we'll turn the ship over and go back."

The effect of Jet's remark was electrifying. The Australian sat up on his couch and, because he wasn't wearing his boots, sailed upwards and came to an abrupt stop as his head hit the underside of the bunk above him. Under different circumstances, it would have been a funny incident but one look at Mitch's face told me this was no moment for hilarity. Angrily he pushed himself down again and grabbed the rail to hold himself in position.

"Go back!" he shouted. "Go back? This ship's not turning back. It started out to land on the Moon and it's going to do it."

Jet had been extremely patient. Over the last twenty hours he had given no sign that he resented Mitch's irritability but now, it seemed, the Australian had gone too far.

"You know as well as I do," shouted Jet, "that to attempt to land without accurate details of our position and velocity would be suicide."

"We're not turning back," repeated Mitch.

"But what if our speed is too high and we use up too much fuel landing on the Moon? How do we get off again?"

"We've got to take a chance."

"Oh no," said Jet conclusively. "Not that kind of chance. I'm not taking any unnecessary risks with the lives of this crew. If the radio isn't working within forty-eight hours, we're turning back."

"We're not turning back."

"Am I the captain of this ship or are you?"

I thought for a moment that Mitch would strike Jet but, while he was still thinking about it, Jet cut in:

"One more word out of you, Mitch, and I'll put you under arrest."

Mitch threw back his head and laughed.

"That's funny, that is. Where do you think you are – at sea? What are you going to do? Put me in irons?"

I thought it was time I intervened. I got off my bunk and stood between the two men.

"Hey Mitch – Jet – break it up," I told them. "You're acting like a couple of school kids."

Much to my surprise, Jet turned on me. "You stay out of this, Doc. If I want your advice I'll ask for it."

"But, Jet . . ."

He didn't let me finish. "Seems we have a case of mutiny on our hands."

"Mutiny? That's great," Mitch yelled.

"What else is it?" demanded Jet. "While I'm captain of this ship you'll do as I say or take the consequences."

That was enough. Mitch didn't say any more. He just stared sullenly at Jet, breathing heavily. Now Jet saw he had control of the situation, he became calmer.

"Right," he said, "we'll forget it. But if I decide to go back, we go back. Is that clear?"

Mitch nodded his head, almost imperceptibly.

"Now," went on Jet, "get out the navigation tables. Then go over to the astrodome and start taking bearings. Maybe having something to do will make you feel better."

It was not the time to say so but I'd been thinking that all along. Had Jet ordered Mitch to take our bearings in the first place, this somewhat ugly scene might well have been avoided. Mitch, still rather reluctantly, set to work.

Jet turned to me. "Doc, you give me a hand will you?"

"Yes, Jet," I said; "what at?"

"At getting a rough idea of our distance from Earth with the help of the radar. It won't be all that accurate but it'll be better than nothing."

An hour later Jet took our findings across to where Mitch was still figuring. I moved over to Lemmy who, I knew, must be feeling more depressed than any of us, and certainly in need of a little encouragement.

"How you doing, Lemmy?" I said as I approached him.

"Oh, hullo, Doc," he replied. "I'm putting it all together again now, and hoping."

"Can I be of any help?"

"Yes, Doc. You can pass me a few things as I ask for them. But be careful – one touch and they go shooting all over the place. Talk about light and airy like a fairy."

I was pleased that in spite of everything Lemmy had not lost his good humour.

"I'll be careful," I told him.

"Then hand me that for a start," he said. I passed a screwdriver over to him.

"Ta," he said as he reached out for it. "And how's the mutiny going?"

"Oh, they seem to have forgotten it now. They've got enough trouble on their hands, trying to work out our position."

"Think they'll do it, Doc?" he asked, seriously.

"I guess so. But it'll take them some time. Our real hope is you, Lemmy – you and the radio."

He didn't reply to that but instead asked: "What made Mitch flare up like that?"

"I don't know. Maybe the thought that he might not get to the Moon after all, or maybe the cramped conditions and lack of gravity have something to do with it. Who can tell? Nobody has ever been in our circumstances before."

The radio was now almost reassembled. Lemmy was just putting the final screws into place when a thought occurred to me.

"Was the recorder switched on during that row, Lemmy?"

He paused for a moment. "Er – no, it wasn't."

"Pity!"

"Eh?"

"I'd have liked to have kept a record of every word spoken during this trip."

"What for?"

"All manner of things can be concluded from the way men act and what they say, and a record of our reactions might help other crews in the future. There must be some reason why two men, perfectly stable on Earth, should jump at each other's throats less than twenty-four hours after leaving it. There was no need for it, Lemmy. It doesn't make sense."

"I'm not jumping at anybody's throat, Doc. Neither are you."

"Not yet you aren't, but watch it. There's no knowing what might happen if you had nothing to do but sit and wait as Jet and Mitch were doing."

Lemmy grunted.

"Fat chance of that."

After a few minutes he looked up from his work and said: "Do you think we should turn back, Doc?"

"Yes," I told him. "Unless you can get that radio working."

"That's what I think, too. Jet was right. Mitch ought to have known better."

"Maybe. But that still doesn't excuse Jet for losing his temper."

"No, I don't suppose it does." He looked over his shoulder at where Mitch and Jet were busy with their tables. "Can they hear what we're saying?"

"If they were listening they might. But at the moment they're too busy to notice us."

"There," said Lemmy as he turned the last screw home. "Now, Doc, we'll try again."

"To raise Control?"

"Yeah."

"What do you think our chances are?"

"I don't know. Three times I've pulled this stuff to pieces and three times I've put it all together again. And each time she should have worked; but even the emergency circuits don't function. I can't understand it. It's got me worried Doc."

"Well, you can't do more than your best."

"But it makes me feel I'm letting the ship down."

"You shouldn't let it get you that way, Lemmy."

"Well, it does. Now, let's switch on and see if we get any juice through her."

He pressed the switch and we both looked hopefully at the current indicators. They sprang to life. I almost shouted in my excitement.

"It's there."

Lemmy was even more excited than I. He laughed as he said: "Yeah – we made it." Then he took control of himself and said: "No, wait, don't let's get too excited. We're not through to home yet."

"Then give them a call, for goodness' sake," I said. "Try to raise them."

Lemmy switched on the microphone and slowly and deliberately chanted:

"Hullo, Control. Rocketship Luna calling Control. If you love me and can hear me, let's hear from you. Over."

Not a sound came from the loudspeaker.

Lemmy made a gesture of disgust with his hands.

"Not a peep," he said. "They should be receiving us, Doc, there's bags of aerial current. They should hear us on Mars with this equipment. Why, if . . ."

He suddenly broke off to look up at the speaker, cock his head to one side and listen. Faintly, very faintly, from the gauze-covered circle came an odd sound.

"Hey," I said, "what's that?"

"I haven't a clue," he replied.

The sound we were hearing could never be adequately described in words. It began as a high-pitched, almost musical note. As it descended, it increased in volume and on its loudest and lowest note it paused, reverberated like the pedal note of a mighty organ in a deep canyon, and then faded out. But before it disappeared a second note was heard. Like its predecessor, it swooped basswards like an imitation of an acrobatic aircraft or the rush of water over a fall.

Then came a third note, a fourth, a fifth; more and more, too many to count, sliding down the whole range of audible frequencies, one just behind the other, each blending harmoniously with the next. A kaleidoscopic pattern of sound, swooping and descending with a slight lift at the end of each run, like the flight of a gull towards the sea.

The overall noise grew louder and Lemmy seemed deeply moved by it. He began to tremble slightly. He licked his lip's and, with his eyes wide open, said: "It gives you the creeps doesn't it?"

"Haven't you any idea what it is, Lemmy?"

"It sounds like music. But music I never heard before."

It *was* like music – music of another age; mysterious, spinechilling, unearthly. I put my ear close to the speaker. Somewhere within that surging, eerie symphony I thought I could detect, very faintly, a voice.

"Can you hear a voice there?" I asked.

I dunno, Doc," Lemmy was extremely agitated. "I can't make it out."

By this time the sound filled the whole cabin. Jet and Mitch looked up from their work in surprise.

"Is the radio working now?" asked Jet, coming over to where Lemmy and I were standing.

"Can you get Control?" queried Mitch.

"She's working all right, and that should be Control you're hearing, but it isn't."

"Are you sure she's on the right frequency, Lemmy?"

"Why shouldn't she be? Impossible for her to drift off, with all those crystal stabilisers in there."

The weird sound emanating from the amplifier had, until then, been loud, but almost as soon as Jet and Mitch reached us it began to fade. Just as Lemmy finished explaining about the crystals, there was a rapid upward surge of sound, culminating in a number of high-pitched, tremulous notes like the harmonics of a thousand violins playing in unison. Then silence.

Lemmy was perspiring. "It's gone. Packed in again." He was so disappointed his eyes filled with tears.

"Call them once more, Lemmy," said Jet gently. "Give them one more try."

There was a break in Lemmy's voice as, for at least the hundredth time, he switched on the microphone.

"Hullo, Earth. Hullo, Control. Rocketship Luna calling. Can you hear us? Come in *please*."

The last sentence he repeated in a tone of desperation. But less than two seconds later his expression changed to one of joy, for from the radio came the clear, calm and familiar voice of Earth.

"Hullo, Luna. Hearing you loud and clear. Strength 4.5."

"It's them. We made it!" Lemmy was doing his best to hop from one foot to the other. Jet pushed him to one side and reached for the mike switch.

"Hullo, Control. This is Morgan. Can you still hear us?"

"Of course we can," came back the reply. "We've been hearing you ever since take-off."

"Eh?" Lemmy stopped his dance. His mouth dropped open in surprise. "You mean you've been hearing us all the time?" he asked incredulously.

"Except when you took the radio to pieces."

Mitch shot an enquiring glance in Lemmy's direction. The voice of Control continued. "There must be something wrong with your receiving circuit."

Mitch was about to speak but before he could get a word out Lemmy, as though appealing to Earth for support, yelled into the microphone:

"But I couldn't find anything wrong – nothing. All I did was take the works to pieces and put them back together again. They're just the same now as when we took off. I can't understand it. It doesn't make sense." He stepped back from the table with a defiant look on his face.

"Well, you're certainly functioning OK now, Luna. Stand by for full details of your position and velocity."

Jet switched on the recorder. "Go ahead, Control. Standing by."

We listened anxiously as the coveted information was slowly and precisely given to us, every figure repeated three times. We were 142,000 miles from Earth and our speed had dropped to 42,000 mph. This was very nearly what it would have been if the firing and cutting off of the second motor had been carried out by Control as originally intended and not by us. We all felt very pleased with ourselves. We became cheerful again, made jokes and went out of our way to be polite to one another.

When Control's long recitation of facts and figures had ended and the operator's recorded voice had been played back to him for final check, our normal working routine went into action.

Watches were divided into four hours per man. Jet took the first, Mitch the second, then me and finally, to enable him to get a long period of sleep without interruption, Lemmy. Leaving Jet at the control table, the rest of us retired to our bunks. The last thing of which I was aware was Jet replaying the log to himself via the reproduction earpiece and copying down the figures for comparison with the estimated flight schedule we had brought with us.

Ten hours later we were having our first leisurely meal together. Lemmy, purely for the novelty of the experience, had taken his on the ceiling, his rations having been floated up to him by gentle pushes. From his lofty position he kept up an almost constant flow of small talk.

"Push me up a banana, will you, Doc? Ta."

"Lemmy, do you always intend to take your meals upside down on the ceiling?" Jet asked him.

"What difference does it make? It all goes down, or should I say 'up', just the same."

"But it looks so undignified."

"Great idea for cocktail parties though. Think of the room it saves."

"Anything more, Lemmy?" I asked.

"No thanks, Doc. I've about eaten my fill."

"Then push your empties down and I'll stow them away."

"How about a little after-dinner music?" came the voice from above.

"Oh, not that, Lemmy," protested Mitch.

"Got to do something to pass the time."

It had been agreed that each man could bring from Earth some purely personal object or objects weighing not more than one pound. I had brought my journal and, at every opportunity, filled its pages with details of our life within the confined space of the ship and our individual reactions to it. Both Jet and Mitch had brought a book apiece; Mitch, a technical treatise on atomic power and Jet, a well-worn copy of a fictional work.

Lemmy had no literary aspirations. He had brought a mouth-organ and, during his off-duty periods, treated us to selections from his repertoire. Unfortunately it wasn't very large; unfortunately too, in our cramped quarters there was no escaping it. At the moment the cabin resounded to the echoes of Lemmy's favourite item, 'Knocked 'em in the Old Kent Road.' He was also very adept at playing Hebrew dances.

We resigned ourselves to suffer in silence. Even Mitch refrained from repeating his objection for, now that we were in radio contact with Earth again, Lemmy was the hero of the hour. But we had endured only a few bars of the old Cockney ballad when it was brought to an abrupt close by a sound like the sharp report of a heavy-bore rifle. It was followed, within a fraction of a second, by the shriek of the klaxon horn which told us we has been struck by a meteor.

We had been drilled for this moment for months. Jet had his drinking straw to his lips, finishing the last of his cold tea. His immediate reaction was to 'drop everything' – and he did. Down on Earth his bottle would have gone crashing to the floor. But not here. It remained where it was, poised in the air.

"Emergency! Action stations!" Jet yelled.

We needed no second bidding. In fact Mitch and I were up on our feet before he got the order out.

"Blimey!" It was Lemmy. "Emergency, and me upside down on the ceiling."

"The space suits!" Jet shouted up at him.

"Don't panic," he replied. "I'm on my way."

I half ran, half floated across to my control panel. There I checked the air pressure and found, to my great relief, that it was constant. At least the ship's inner shell had not been holed. I announced the fact to Jet.

"The meteor bumper must have worked," yelled Mitch above the noise of the klaxon.

"That we'll see. Put your suits on anyway," said Jet, taking his from Lemmy who was now handing them round. "Put on your helmets, too, but don't fasten them."

I stayed at my post by the air pressure indicator, ready to press the siren should the needle begin to waver.

Jet turned off the shrieking buzzer. Then Mitch, from his place at the engineering panel, announced: "Fuel tanks and motor seem to be intact. No damage there according to the board."

"Good. Right, Lemmy. Call up base. Report this to Control immediately."

"Yes, Jet."

Fifteen minutes later we were still at our posts but none of the indicators gave us any sign that the ship had suffered any serious damage. An hour later vigilance was relaxed, but it was essential to know what damage, however slight, the ship had sustained. There was only one way to find out and that was to go outside and look.

"Outside?" asked Lemmy. "Into – *nothing*?"

"Only one of us needs to – I'll go," said Jet.

"No, let me," said Mitch.

I tried to put my spoke in.

"Oh no, Mitch, this is my job. If anything should go wrong, should the suits break down or anything unforeseen happen, you are of far more importance to the crew than I."

"Do you mean that whoever goes out there has a chance of not coming back again?" Lemmy swallowed.

"It's possible, Lemmy. It will be the first time any man has ever been out there – in true space. His life will depend principally on the efficiency of the suit he's wearing. And as I designed these suits," I turned to Jet, "it follows that I should be the one to put them to the test."

"You tested them on Earth, Doc, didn't you?"

"Of course, as far as I could. But this will be different, Jet – the real thing."

The fact was that, with the exception of Lemmy, we were all itching to go outside. Jet decided to draw lots for it, Lemmy included. Jet won.

Still wearing our suits, but without helmets, we prepared to let him out of the cabin, into the airlock and through the main door. Air was first let into the lock to fill up the vacuum. It rushed in with a loud hiss that could be heard through the cabin floor. Next the hatchway was opened and, when it had reached full aperture, Jet descended the ladder into the small, airtight compartment below. He looked up at the three of us glancing down at him and grinned.

"All right, Doc," he said. "Close the hatch."

I closed her and Jet was lost to view. Lemmy had already turned on the ship's intercom radio that would keep us in touch with Jet while he was outside. Soon we heard the rattle of his throat mike as he switched it on.

"Over to intercom," said his voice, now coming from the loudspeaker. "Fastening helmet."

"Hearing you loud and clear," said Lemmy.

"Helmet fastened. Exhaust the lock."

There was a click of relays and a long, sustained hiss of air as the airlock slowly emptied.

"Suit now inflating," came Jet's voice.

"Air pressure zero," I announced.

"Then open the door and turn me loose."

It opened, the electric motors filling the cabin with a deep, musical hum. When it ceased we heard quite distinctly, an exclamation of surprise.

"What is it, Jet – something wrong?" asked Mitch.

"It's more beautiful than I ever dreamed."

"What is?"

"The stars. Millions upon millions of them." His voice now took on a matter-of-fact tone. "Am now leaving door and walking up side of ship. I'll make a complete circuit."

"How's the suit, Jet?" I asked him.

"Fine, Doc, fine. More comfortable than I'd dared to hope. Now hitching safety line and walking towards nose."

I could imagine him out there, walking up the side of the ship like a fly up a wall. To him 'down' was towards his feet –

whatever part of the ship he might be. If, by any mischance, his magnetic boots failed and he went drifting off into the void, his safety line would hold and enable him to pull himself back.

"Any sign of where the meteor hit us?" It was Mitch.

"No, not yet."

"Ask him if he can see the Earth," prompted Lemmy.

"Not now," Mitch replied. "One thing at a time. Finding the point of impact is more important."

But Jet had already found it. The meteor had struck us near the ship's nose. Apparently it must have been a very small one – minute – for only a tiny part of the steel outer casing had vaporised. We thanked our lucky stars it hadn't been larger.

We all now expected Jet to make his way back to the airlock and return to the cabin. But no.

"You must come out here, all of you," he said with bated breath. "This is something you've got to see."

"We can't all go," Mitch told him. "Somebody must stay to work the airlock."

In spite of my great desire to join Jet outside the ship, I volunteered to remain behind, asking, by way of compensation, that I should be the first to step down on the surface of the Moon. My request was granted. A few moments later Mitch and Lemmy were outside with Jet and I could hear their excited voices as they pointed out to one another the sights of the universe.

"Did you ever see so many stars? So many different colours, too. And so small and bright," said Lemmy. "How fast are we going, Jet?"

"About 2,000 miles an hour."

"We don't seem to be moving at all."

"Take a look at the Moon, Lemmy. Even from this distance you can see the mountains and craters on her."

"How far away is she now?"

"At a rough guess I'd say about a hundred thousand miles."

"Oh. No distance at all. A fourpenny bus ride."

"If it's a sight you want to see, take a look at the Earth." Mitch had joined the conversation now. "You can make out the African continent quite easily and the reflection from the ice cap is almost too brilliant to look at."

"If we never get to the Moon," said Jet, "the trip will have been worth it – just for this."

"Jet," said Lemmy, "I'm going for a walk down under."

"Then be sure your safety line is secure. We don't want you drifting off."

"Don't worry, boy. I don't aim to leave this ship yet. You must come out here, Doc, you'd enjoy it. Maybe when I've taken my constitutional I'll come in and you can come out."

"Thanks, Lemmy," I told him. "I'd like to."

I visualized them out there, stuck to the hull of the rocket; Jet and Mitch standing on one side and Lemmy walking away from them down to the opposite side. Lemmy was still talking, half to me, half to himself.

"If only Becky could see me now, she wouldn't know if I was on my head or my heels – any more than I do. Do you know, Doc . . ." He paused. "Huh?" he said, as though Jet or Mitch had spoken, "what's that?" But neither of them had said a word, and I certainly hadn't as I'd been listening to Lemmy. But he had heard something for he went on: "There it is again – that funny music."

I listened intently but could hear nothing. "What is it, Lemmy?" I asked him. "What can you hear?"

He didn't reply but continued talking to himself. "There it is again." He began to sound alarmed. "And getting louder. Doc, can you hear me? Why don't you answer?"

"I *am* answering you, Lemmy – what is it?" But although I could hear Lemmy all right, he obviously couldn't hear me. Urgently he called Jet, but didn't hear when he replied either. Now that I knew Jet was trying to contact him, I shut up. Too many voices would only have confused the issue.

But Lemmy wasn't hearing anybody. And with me in the cabin and Jet and Mitch on the far side of the ship, nobody could see him or have any way of finding out what was wrong. The Cockney was near to panic now. He yelled for Jet half a dozen times, each call louder than the last until his final call was little less than a scream. Suddenly contact was re-established for, in response to Jet's repeated demands to know what was wrong, Lemmy cried breathlessly: "That music. Didn't you hear it?"

"Music? What music?"

"But you must have heard it. It sounded as though it was right inside my helmet."

"Lemmy, pull yourself together," Jet commanded. "I heard no music. I heard nothing but your yelling and screaming."

"But I was calling you before that. Didn't you hear me?"

"Yes, and we replied. Now stay where you are, Lemmy. Don't attempt to enter the ship until I'm alongside you."

Chapter 6
MEN ON THE MOON

I shall never forget the sight of Lemmy as he came up out of the airlock. He had removed his helmet before he climbed the ladder: "to get a breath of air," he said, although the air in the cabin was little different from that breathed in the suits; there was just more of it. His face was white and covered in perspiration. His eyes were glassy and he was trembling. Whatever he had heard out there, whatever it was that had happened, it had obviously frightened him very much.

I was all for letting him lie on his bunk to get over his shock, but Jet and Mitch, particularly Mitch, wanted to question him first. I protested, but Jet decided that a few questions now, while the experience was still fresh in Lemmy's mind, would be more valuable.

All that Lemmy could say was that he had heard the weird music again and that it had 'scared the living daylights out of him'. It had been stronger than before and had seemed to get 'right inside' him until he had felt sick and dizzy and was certain he would faint. That was when he began calling for me and then, receiving no answer, for Jet.

"Look, Lemmy," said Jet, after listening to Lemmy's version of the matter, "if there had been any noise, or music, as you call it, it must have been coming over your radio and we should have heard it, too."

"Then if it didn't come over the radio, where did it come from?"

No one answered this question. None of us would voice the first thought that came into all our minds, not in front of Lemmy anyway. But he was no fool.

"Oh," he said, "so you think I imagined it. Think maybe I'm going crackers, got a screw loose somewhere. Well, I'm not, see. I heard it, I tell you, as clear as I can see you sitting there."

"Then why didn't you call us – tell us to listen out for it, too?" asked Mitch.

"I did. I called Doc the minute I heard it. But he didn't answer. Then I called Jet, but he didn't answer either – not until the noise stopped."

Lemmy was still very agitated and, in his efforts to convince us of the truth of his story, was becoming even more worked up, shouting his replies at the top of his voice. I could see the danger signal and, in spite of Jet's and Mitch's objections, I, as ship's doctor, insisted that he be questioned no more.

"Come along, Lemmy, you need sleep. It'll make you feel a lot better," I said, not, I'm afraid, with much conviction.

He reluctantly allowed me to lead him to his bunk. "But I don't need sleep. They don't believe me, do they, Doc? Neither of 'em. But you do. You heard that weird music coming over the radio, didn't you?" he pleaded.

"No, Lemmy, I didn't. I wasn't even out there."

My remark seemed to be the last straw. The whole ship was against him. He let me strap him into his bunk without further protest. I gave him one of my magic pills (his term for them) and, having seen him comfortably settled, rejoined Jet and Mitch at the central table.

Jet was worried. "What has happened to him?" he was asking Mitch.

"What do you think has happened to him? The strain is too much for him, that's what. He's cracking up."

I thought this unfair, particularly as it had not yet been proved whether Lemmy had heard the noise or not. Jet was more generous. He knew Lemmy far better than Mitch or I and, in consequence, was less hasty in jumping to conclusions.

"If Lemmy says he heard a strange noise, then he heard it," said Jet.

"Then why didn't I hear it? Or you, or Doc?"

"Doc wasn't outside."

"He was listening on the ship's radio, wasn't he? And we were all on the same frequency. Lemmy must have imagined the whole thing. What other explanation is there?"

"Who knows? Anything might happen out here. Radios could play tricks – Lemmy's, the ship's, anybody's."

"Piffle!"

Jet turned to me. "What's your opinion, Doc?"

I told him I would like to reserve it. It seemed to me that Lemmy was suffering from acute claustrophobia when he re-entered the ship and couldn't get out of his suit quickly enough. This might account for a slight mental upset; and, the noise we had heard through the radio still in his mind, he might well have imagined he was hearing it all over again. But if this were a true explanation, it was a strange one, for Lemmy was not the type to be upset by enclosed spaces.

As I finished talking, Lemmy's voice came from his bunk over on the far side of the cabin.

"I can hear you."

Apparently the pills I had given him had nor yet taken effect. Jet moved that we should adjourn the discussion until Lemmy was asleep.

"The trouble with this ship," he added, "is that room's so limited you can hardly keep your thoughts to yourself."

"Next time I'll build separate cabins," said Mitch sarcastically; "first, second, and tourist class."

Tempers were getting frayed again so I hastily changed the subject back to the one we were supposed to be discussing.

"I really don't know what to think. We all heard those peculiar, almost frightening sounds coming from the radio before we finally contacted Control."

"Atmospherics." Mitch brought his fist down on the table as he spoke.

"What, on *this* equipment?" Jet swept his arm towards the radio. "That music was too strong, too pure to be atmospherics."

"You'll be saying next that it was transmitted."

"Could be."

Mitch sneered. "Where from? The Moon?"

"Why not?"

"Because there's no life on the Moon, that's why."

"How do you know?"

"Good heavens, Jet, what's got into you? Any fool knows the Moon is dead. There's no life on it of any kind."

"Not on the Earth side, I grant you," I said, "but what about the other side?"

Mitch turned on me impatiently. "Are you also trying to say there is life on the Moon and that noise was transmitted from there?"

"Well, you can't rule out the possibility," I said.

"*I* can. Life on the Moon is out of the question. Chances of life on other planets, extremely remote. But all this is apart from the point; it's Lemmy we're supposed to be discussing. What are we going to do about him?"

"What do you suggest?" I asked, with some misgivings.

"For a start we'll make it a rule he doesn't leave the ship again."

"Nobody will be leaving the ship again," said Jet. "Not until the landing is made."

"I don't mean while we're still coasting, I mean from now on. Even after we've touched down."

"I can still hear you," came Lemmy's rather pathetic voice from the isolation of his bunk.

Jet ignored him. "What? You mean you'd let him go all the way and then deny him the right even to step outside?"

"Yes, unless we can be a hundred per cent sure we won't get a repeat performance of what happened half an hour ago."

"I wouldn't do it to him."

"And neither would I," I added.

"I tell you Lemmy is unstable. He'll be seeing Moonmen next, with antennae – and one eye in the middle of their foreheads."

"Mitch," said Jet, "you are being unreasonable."

"I just want to be sure that nothing wrecks this project, that's all."

"That's more important to you than anything – or anyone, isn't it?" Anger blazed in Jet's eyes.

"You're darned right it is."

There was a pause.

"Sorry, Mitch. Lemmy carries on as before," said Jet firmly. "What happened outside makes no difference."

"All right. I'll consider myself overruled, but let's hope I never have to say 'I told you so'."

And there, for the time being, the matter rested. I looked over at Lemmy. The drugs had taken their effect. He was fast asleep. When he awoke, Lemmy was his normal self again and although, once more, the ship settled down to routine, I was disturbed to realise that our tempers and judgment could be upset so easily.

There was little for us to do during coasting. Periodically we called up Control to check our height, speed and decreasing velocity. When not on watch, Mitch studied his tables, Jet read his novel, I filled in my journal and Lemmy played his mouth-organ. Soon the most dangerous part of our trip would be upon us: the Moon landing, something we had never been able to practise on Earth.

We passed neutral gravitation point exactly three Earth days, seven hours and six minutes after take-off. Speed was then only a few miles per hour. Now we were no longer under the influence of the Earth's pull. We were falling towards the Moon, and our velocity began to increase.

The Moon was 23,000 miles away and the time had come for us to turn the ship over. At zero hour, we strapped ourselves onto our couches, turned on the gyros and slowly, very slowly, almost imperceptibly at first, the ship began to turn. After what seemed an eternity, the manoeuvre was completed; our nose pointing towards Earth and our stern towards the Moon for, to make the landing, which entailed using the rocket-motor as a brake, it was necessary to drop towards the Moon backwards.

Soon its image more than filled our screen. The familiar Bay of Rainbows, where we were to land, showed in detail; every crater, mountain, crevice, crack and chasm being clearly visible although, at this height, still fairly small. When we were a thousand miles above the Bay we prepared to make the landing.

Once more we strapped ourselves into our bunks. We were dead on course. The televiewers were glowing above our heads. We were playing with death, we realised that, but this did not dampen our spirits and least of all did it subdue Lemmy's natural cheerfulness which, by now, was fully restored to him.

"If there's a man on the Moon," he said, "I hope he's put the kettle on. I could just do with a hot cup of tea."

"Let's hope we don't hit her too hard," was Mitch's only comment.

"Safety straps fastened?" came Jet's cold enquiry.

"OK," we all replied.

"Doc, stabiliser."

I switched on the gyro.

"Lemmy, course?"

"Spot on."

"Mitch, height?"

"950 miles."

"Shock absorbers ready?"

"Yes, Jet."

"Let's hope they can stand the concussion." That was Jet's only personal comment during landing preparations.

"They will," said Mitch.

"Contact!"

Mitch pressed the switch and there was a heavy, whirring sound as the four great shock absorbers housed in the stern slowly positioned themselves outside the ship. Height was now 910 miles.

"Still some way to fall yet," said Jet. "Relax; gravity conditions will return as soon as the motor is cut in. Don't let the shock take you by surprise."

"Height, 900 miles."

"Blimey." It was Lemmy. He was looking at his televiewer screen. "We're not going to land on that lot, are we?"

"No, Lemmy," said Jet, "they're the mountains that surround the Bay. Where we're landing is much smoother."

"It'd better be."

"Height, 895."

"Landing area still spot on."

"890."

"Huh? What's that?" said Lemmy.

"What's what?" asked Jet.

"Quiet, Lemmy," said Mitch.

"Height, 880."

"Jet, I can hear . . ."

"What *is* it, Lemmy?" said Jet.

"Height, 875."

"Nothing." The tone of Lemmy's voice belied him. "It's the excitement, I . . ."

"For heaven's sake, what's wrong?"

Lemmy's reply was desperate. "Nothing, nothing, I tell you. Take no notice."

"Height, 870."

"Stand by to cut in the motor."

Lemmy was almost in tears. "Landing area still spot on."

Mitch yelled at him: "Lemmy, pull yourself together."

"865 – 860 – 855 – 850."

"Contact!" yelled Jet.

The ship vibrated as the atomic motor exploded into life. The speed of our fall decreased and we could feel the pressure as gravity returned to the ship, centred towards its nose. Had we not been strapped in we would, of course, all have hit the ceiling.

Slowly, slowly we descended.

600 miles – 500 – 400. Soon it was only 200 – 100 – 90 – 70 – 50 – 30 – 20 – 10 . . .

"Here she comes," said Mitch.

"This is it," said Jet. "Hold tight."

On the televiewer above my head the view of the Moon was blotted out by the flaming exhaust as it rebounded off the Moon's surface. There was a crump and a jolt. I held my breath. The ship rocked a little. For a moment I thought she might topple over. But no, she was steady. We had made it.

This was a stupendous moment – a moment, it would have seemed, for wild excitement, but all we did was to remain lying on our bunks – in silence; a silence that was broken by a calm understatement from Jet as he announced: "Gentlemen, we're on the Moon."

Nobody replied. Not at first. And then Mitch, his voice trembling slightly, said:

"Didn't you hear what Jet said? We've just landed on the Moon." There was a longer pause while Mitch waited for some reaction. "Doc, Lemmy – didn't you hear?"

"I heard him," said Lemmy. He didn't sound at all excited.

"And so did I," I announced without much more enthusiasm.

"But doesn't that mean anything to you? The way you're carrying on, Jet might just have announced your death sentence."

I don't know why I felt so depressed, but I did.

"Maybe he has," I replied.

Now it was Jet's turn to be puzzled.

"What's up, Doc?" he said. "And, Lemmy – what's worrying you?"

"Nothing."

"Out with it, Lemmy," said Jet firmly.

Mitch joined in, his voice tinged with anger. "You didn't hear that darned music again, did you?"

"Leave me alone," said Lemmy. "Why do you keep getting at me all the time?"

"You did hear it or, at least, you think you did. Am I right? Am I?"

"Oh, leave him alone, Mitch," I said.

Instead he turned on me. "In a minute I expect you'll be saying you heard it, too."

"I'm not so sure that I didn't," I told him.

"What?" said Jet. "You, too, Doc?"

I couldn't be sure. But just before the motor was switched on I had begun to feel very strange. A sense of great foreboding gripped me. I tried to explain this.

"Well, with the landing only a few minutes away," said Jet, "how else would you feel?"

"It wasn't that," I began to say. "I didn't exactly hear anything but . . ."

"I know," said Mitch sarcastically, "you just felt it."

"Yes," I said, "that's the only way I can describe it."

"Now you're both beginning to imagine things, you and Lemmy."

"Mitch," I said, "it was not imagination."

"Well," Jet broke in, "let's forget it. We've got work to do and little time in which to do it. Now get up and we'll start."

Lemmy, still unhappy, began to put his magnetised boots on.

"You won't need those, Lemmy," called Jet. "Not until we return. Have you forgotten there's gravity on the Moon? Now switch on the main televiewer and we'll see what it looks like outside."

Lemmy turned the televiewer on and the large screen over the control table lit up. Outside, in glaring sunlight, clear in every detail, was the Moon's surface.

The Bay of Rainbows, in which we had landed, is situated in the north-east quadrant of the Moon-globe. It lies to the north of Mare Imbrium (the Sea of Rains) and can, on good 'seeing' nights on Earth, be seen with the naked eye. Through binoculars it stands out clearly, the darker surface of the 'sea' contrasting strongly with the lighter-coloured mountains that border its northern shore. The Bay is guarded by two promontories, Laplace and Heraclides, the shore of the Bay running from one to the other in an almost perfect semi-circle.

Laplace and Heraclides form part of the Jura Mountains which rise out of the sea and reach their highest altitude, 29,000 feet, halfway round the Bay. Laplace is steep and reaches 9,000 feet while Heraclides reaches only 4,500 – for a Moon mountain, not particularly high.

We landed in the sunlight but, only a few hours before, the landing area had been in darkness for the Moon's terminator was moving westwards away from us – to return again from the east in fourteen Earth days' time. The purpose of landing so early in the lunar morning was to give us the maximum possible time in sunlight before the long darkness again overtook the Bay and compelled us to return home.

Towering above the horizon in the picture on the televiewer screen was Cape Laplace, its uppermost peaks bathed in the sunlight, throwing a great, long, pointed, razor-edged shadow across the level plain of the Bay. Perhaps 'level' is hardly the right word. I don't believe there is one true level spot anywhere on the Moon. The 'sea' that forms the Bay is solidified lava, with a surface like pie-crust – low, easy swells, narrow, shallow cracks and numerous small craters which, in the bright sun, stood out in sharp relief.

The Jura Mountains, which surrounded us on three sides, reached incredible heights: 20,000 feet at their maximum. It was as though we had landed at the foot of the Himalayas. But the most incredible thing was the sky. It was black and the stars shone out of it by the million; stars invisible on Earth being as easily discernible as those of first magnitude, even over that part of the bay on which the sun was shining. It was neither night nor day. It was one and the same – together. The sunlit cliffs, seen against the black sky, seemed to be floodlit from below rather than illuminated from above.

We took a look at the sun as it rose above the peaks of Cape Laplace. It was a bluish white and, as it came over the horizon, the long streaks of its prominences were as clear as during a total eclipse down on Earth.

Everywhere was barrenness, loneliness, utter desolation. Even inside the ship we could sense the deep, awful silence without. We pointed out objects to each other in hushed voices. Then, by means of the televiewer, we made a tour of the Bay, from dark Heraclides to sunlit Laplace. Our trip completed, we shut off the televiewer, opened up the radio and called Control to tell them that our journey was over and we had made a safe landing.

Everybody knows what happened then. Every radio station in the world relayed our conversation with Control. For half an hour we answered questions from the ABC commentator in Luna City down, or should I say 'up', there in Australia. Every word we said was reported in every principal newspaper on Earth. We described the bleakness, the loneliness, the almost monochromatic world that was the Moon. We spoke to Sydney and New York and answered, as best we could, the questions relayed to us. Then, still hooked up to Luna City and the world in general, the first attempt to leave the ship and descend to the Moon's surface was made.

It was Lemmy's turn to stay inside. In great anticipation, Jet, Mitch and I donned our space suits, went through the airlock and, after the ladder had been extended, made our way down its rungs towards the Moon's surface with Mitch leading. In spite of Mitch's offer that I could be the first to step on to the Moon, when it came to it I conceded the honour to him. For Mitch was like a child, he was so excited. He went down well ahead of Jet and we could hear his heavy breathing over our personal radios.

"I feel so light and the going's so easy, I want to let go and float down."

"No, Mitch," said Jet anxiously. "Don't run any risks, take it easy."

We waited for him to reach the surface.

"Well, I made it."

"How does it feel?" asked Jet.

"Fine, except that I'm ankle deep in dust. Be careful how you walk, the ground's full of cracks and mounds."

I looked down and saw Mitch walking rapidly round in circles. In a minute or two Jet had joined him and they both disappeared out of sight round the ship.

"We can see the Earth now, Doc," came Mitch's voice.

"Come on. Come and look."

"Give me a chance to get down first," I told him. "You two are much too fast for me."

As I left the ladder I heard Jet say: "Hullo, Earth. I can see you now. A great ball in the sky. About twelve times the size that the Moon looks to you."

"Can you pick out the seas and continents?" came the voice of Earth. We could, of course.

Jet was still describing the scene when I caught up with him and Mitch. It was then that we spoke to London. London told us that it was a clear, cloudless evening (we could see for ourselves that all Europe was enjoying unusually clear weather) and that crowds of people were standing in the streets looking up at the Moon and trying to make out the Bay of Rainbows with field glasses and small portable telescopes.

The excitement and exchanges lasted nearly three hours altogether. But at last the interviews, the fun and the laughter were over and we were finally allowed to return to the ship and set about organising the serious work.

Anyone who thinks a fourteen-day sojourn on the Moon would be either pleasurable, thrilling or adventurous had better reconsider his views. Nothing could be duller, unless you happen to be an enthusiastic mineralogist or something of that kind. None of us were. We had our work to do; we had been trained for it, of course, but collecting specimens of moon rock and soil, measuring radioactivity and carrying out surveys for the selenographers down on Earth was, although interesting enough at first, soon a matter of dull routine.

The most enjoyable tasks were connected with the astronomical work. The sun, the stars and the planets were all photographed in their turn; and what wonderful sights they were, the moons of Jupiter and the sun's corona being visible to the unaided eye.

The most unpleasant thing we had to contend with was the heat. We had landed on a part of the Moon where, it was expected, temperature would be akin to that of the tropics down on Earth. In fact, it was slightly higher than that, somewhere in the region of 125°F. If you can imagine yourself in a lifeless desert, with no night, only day, doing hard, physical work clad in a diving suit, you'll have a good idea of the kind of conditions in which we found ourselves.

Our suits carried their own cooling systems but, unfortunately, these were not as effective as we had hoped. When we first left the ship we were comfortable enough, the temperature inside our suits being between 65 and 70 degrees. But we had only to walk in the sun for a few minutes to find the temperature rising rapidly. Within an hour it was unbearable and we either had to return to the ship or seek the shade. Then within a few minutes, we would be cool enough to venture out into the light again. But as the sun rose higher in the lunar heavens and noon approached, shady nooks became fewer and our stays outside the ship shorter.

Six days after landing, all shade had virtually disappeared. This meant no one could spend more than an hour outside, including the time it took him to reach the scene of operations and get back again. This reduced each man's actual working time to a mere few minutes. But we did our best and, I must admit, achieved quite a lot under the circumstances. Twice a day we gathered inside the ship for meals and eight hours out of every twenty-four were spent resting. What with sorting and classifying the specimens, reporting our findings to base and reorganising the exploration schedule according to Control's instructions, we had very little time to ourselves and no time at all, you might say, to enjoy the scenery.

The novelty of being in the centre of a moonscape where harsh, sharp-edged, deep shadows stood out in vivid contrast to the illuminated areas, where, in spite of the sunlight, the sky was always black and the stars always visible, soon wore off. We soon came to regard the Moon as an unfriendly, indeed extremely hostile planet where any kind of life was unwelcome. We were all looking forward to our return. The first thing we did each day when, armed with charts, theodolite, telescopic camera or other equipment, we left the ship to carry out our work under the fierce sun, was to glance at the waning Earth hanging in the sky. She looked so cool and friendly. We were all longing to go home.

In spite of the dullness, the exploratory routine was not without incident. First day out, Lemmy discovered that the low gravitational pull allowed him to clear greater heights than an Olympic champion. He startled us all by easily clearing a rock more than twenty feet high. The sensation pleased him so much he would have tried an ever higher one had not Jet commanded him to stop. The risk of accident was too great for that kind of game.

The second incident was far more serious. Mitch was out with Jet at the time. Luna had not landed on the exact spot intended. We were about 5,000 yards out, in fact. Considering that our aim had been made from earth, nearly 242,000 miles away, that wasn't too bad. But the miscalculation meant that our area of exploration had to be changed slightly, which was why we were continually receiving modifications to the schedule from Control.

Less than a hundred yards from us was a crater which, because of its peculiar shape, we were ordered to examine. We were to photograph it and extract soil and rock specimens from the rim, but not to go down into it unless instructed. Jet and Mitch undertook the preliminary survey while I remained on watch in the ship and Lemmy rested.

I watched them both approach the crater. It was quite a small one, being only about seventy feet in diameter and some twenty-five feet in depth. Its walls sloped gently downwards and inwards, giving the object the appearance of a washbowl. It even had a 'plughole' in its centre, about ten feet in diameter. So far as we could see, the hole was the opening to a well-like shaft, but how deep it went or what lay in its bottom we had no means of telling without closer examination. Its rim, although a little crumbly in places, was almost perfectly circular, with a few large boulders resting on it here and there. Bright streaks, almost white in colour and contrasting strongly with the grey of the lava-covered Bay, ran from the rim in every direction. The closer they were to the crater, the brighter they looked. As they got further from it, they grew fainter until, a quarter of a mile away they faded out altogether.

Jet and Mitch reached the rim and set about their work; Jet to collect samples of lava dust and Mitch to knock off chips of rock from one of the boulders. I kept them in view of the television camera and watched their every move. Jet had squatted down, rather awkwardly, in his space suit, while Mitch, holding on to the rock with one hand, began to work his way round to the inner side of the boulder. He was, I thought, taking unnecessary risks and I quietly brought his attention to the fact via the radio.

"Don't worry, Doc," the voice came back. "There are plenty of foot and hand holds. Rock this side is streaked with red and yellow veins. Fellows up on Earth'd be glad to see a sample. Besides . . ."

He got no further. The edge of the rim on which he was standing gave way beneath him. He toppled backwards, headlong into the crater.

He fell in slow motion. There was a good six feet between Mitch and the sloping crater wall directly below him. Enclosed in his pressurised suit, he bounced slowly, like a balloon. Three feet further down he bounced again and started rolling towards the shaft.

I was so scared for him I couldn't speak. Lemmy, sitting crosslegged on his bunk, was unaware of the crisis. He was singing to himself, a parody of his own, 'By the light of the silvery Earth', but was having trouble getting his lines to rhyme. Jet didn't move, or speak, but watched Mitch roll slowly towards the shaft as though fascinated by the spectacle. By some miracle, Mitch came to rest within three feet of the 'plughole', and there he lay; spreadeagled, motionless. I thought, at first, that he must be hurt, for he just lay still. Then it occurred to me that he might have punctured his suit and his air was escaping. If it was, there was little hope for him; if his suit collapsed his lungs would explode, long before we could get him out of the crater and into the safety of the ship's airlock.

"Keep calm, Mitch, and don't move." Jet was talking to him. "If you can hear me and can reply, do so, but don't move."

A grunt was all the reply we got.

Jet was standing up now and removing his safety line from its fastener on his suit. "If you can understand what I'm saying," said Jet's voice softly, "grunt again." Mitch grunted. Jet told the Australian what he was about to do, and then threw the end of his safety line towards Mitch. It landed near his outstretched arm. He picked it up with difficulty in his gloved hand. Then, very gingerly, he rose to his feet and, with Jet pulling firmly, Mitch walked up the sloping walls of the crater.

Ten minutes later he was back in the ship. After detailed examination, his suit and radio proved to be undamaged and Mitch himself had sustained no physical hurt. But it was a near thing and, although we didn't realise it then, only the first of the shocks we were to receive in connection with the 'washbowl'.

The time drew near for returning to Earth. As the lunar day drew to a close and the heat subsided, we were able to stay outside for longer periods. Then, towards evening, we noticed that the terminator had already darkened Cape Laplace and would soon be making its way across the Bay. We were to leave before darkness descended on the landing area so, while Mitch and Jet made their final survey, Lemmy and I got the ship ready for take-off. Six hours later, all specimens had been safely stowed. Motor, radio, radar and the rest of the gear checked, we climbed on to our couches while Jet told Control we were about to leave, and would not be calling them again until we were coasting towards Earth. Then he, too, climbed into his bunk and we were all set.

Lemmy switched on the televiewer camera in the nose, rotated it and gave us one last look at the Bay. The west side was in darkness but Cape Heraclides, still lit by the slowly setting sun, was bright enough, although deep shadows were already appearing to mark the places where the sun failed to reach the precipitous mountain walls.

Then we saw the flag. We had hoisted it the day we arrived. The mast, a lightweight, telescopic affair, had been thrust into the soft, dusty soil of a small mound and held in place by superfine guy ropes that were invisible on the screen. The flag hung limp against the pole. Since we had hoisted it, it had never once moved. It was the last thing we saw before the televiewer was switched over to stern view for the take-off. Soon we would be gone and only the flag, the scorched ground, prints in the dust and the impression of Mitch where he had lain in the washbowl would remain to show we had set foot on the Moon. No wind or rain would ever rub them out. They would stay forever, just as we left them, until some great moonquake destroyed them or the satellite itself was no more.

My thoughts were interrupted by Lemmy's laugh.

"Well, that wasn't so bad, was it?" he said. "Maybe I'll spend my holidays here again. But I'll find better digs next time."

We all joined in his laughter and then, when Jet gave his first order for take-off, became serious again.

"Doc, gyro."

We could feel it rotating. The ship was coming to life. She seemed almost as pleased about going home as we were.

"Stand by for count-off."

"We're going home," whispered Lemmy.

"But we'll be back," said Mitch.

"Firing in 15 seconds."

Nobody spoke now. Take-off would not be so unpleasant as it had been from Earth but, our bodies having got used to the low gravitational pull of the Moon, it would be bad enough.

"Ten seconds."

I set myself to watch the televiewer screen. All the picture showed at the moment was a stabilising fin and part of the Moon's surface below it. But I wanted to see the Bay below us, receding and getting smaller as we pulled away from it.

"5, 4, 3, 2, 1 – fire!"

I tensed slightly, waiting for the roar of the motor to come pulsating through the aluminium frame of my bunk. But nothing happened. Only the slight feel of the big gyro.

"Well, press the ignition switch," said Mitch.

"I did," replied Jet. "Nothing happened."

"Press it again."

A pause.

"Still nothing."

"Hey, Jet." It was Lemmy now. "The radar – it's cut."

The picture on the miniature screen above my head blurred, darkened, and went out.

"Now the televiewer's gone."

The pitch of the gyro began to drop.

"Now the gyro."

The note reached its lowest pitch and faded out altogether. The lights went out. We were plunged into deep, impenetrable darkness.

"Everything's stopped," came Jet's voice from the bunk above. I could hear him pressing buttons. "There's not a thing in the ship that works."

Chapter 7
THE DEAD SHIP

"What's happened to the emergency lights?" Mitch's voice enquired out of the darkness. "They should come on automatically."

"Lemmy."

"Yes, Jet."

"The flashlight hanging behind you. Can you find it?"

"I think so."

"Then switch it on. Hurry. Switch it on."

We could hear Lemmy fumbling. Then the beam from the flashlight stabbed the gloom.

"Thank goodness," I said almost involuntarily. "To lie in the dark as well would be the last straw."

"What do you think has happened, Mitch?" asked Jet.

"Main power supply must have failed. We can thank our lucky stars it didn't happen while we were actually taking off."

"Didn't you inspect the power pack, Lemmy?" asked Jet.

"Of course I did," replied Lemmy indignantly.

"Well, we'd better get down into the hold and check it again. Get the tool pack out of the locker."

Lemmy started to climb out of his bunk.

"And get Mitch's flashlight and mine, too."

"Yes, Jet," said Lemmy meekly.

"And Doc, go round to every control and switch it off. Break every circuit and keep it open until we get back."

Much to Lemmy's disgust, Jet, taking Mitch with him, went down into the hold to inspect the power pack himself. Lemmy and I waited up in the cabin; we were still waiting four hours later.

"How much longer are they going to be?" Lemmy said at last.

"Give them time," I told him. "Dismantling the power pack is a tricky job and it can't be done in five minutes."

"But they've never taken this long to check it before."

"It's never packed in before," I reminded him.

Our conversation was interrupted by the sound of footsteps ascending the iron ladder. A moment later Jet's head popped out of the hole.

"Well, Jet?" I asked.

"Nothing wrong," he said, "so far as we can tell."

Lemmy's face lit up. "Well, thank goodness for that," he said. "Shall I start switching on again?"

"Nothing *wrong*," repeated Jet, "but she doesn't work."

"Huh?" said Lemmy, unable to believe his ears.

"She's as dead as a doornail." Jet sat down, wearily. Then Mitch came up the ladder.

"Is that right, Mitch?" I queried.

"Yes, Doc," he said as he stepped on to the cabin floor. "It beats me."

"The fault must be somewhere else," said Jet. "Up here in the cabin."

"The main distributor board?" I suggested.

"Maybe. We'll look at that next, anyway. And while we're about it you and Lemmy had better start checking your own control boards. See if you find any trouble there."

The new inspection went on for more than an hour, and at the end of it the only conclusion we could come to was that everything should be working but wasn't. All our efforts had proved was that everything was intact but lacked the power necessary to bring it to life. We stood there in the centre of the cabin in the pale light of the one flashlamp still hanging above Lemmy's bunk. We were all waiting for Jet's next move. There wasn't one. All he said was:

"Well, gentlemen, until we trace the trouble we're stuck, stranded. We can't take off. We can't even go outside – the airlock doesn't work either."

"Blimey."

"Then what do we do?" I asked.

Jet took a deep breath. "Look again," he said. "We'll go over every inch of the ship with a fine-tooth comb. Unless we find what's wrong and put it right, we'll be here for ever."

And so the long, weary round of check and counter-check began a second time, and then a third, and then a fourth. Forty-eight hours later we were still at it and no nearer a solution for all our trouble. I thought it was time we took a rest and told Jet so.

"How can we?" he asked.

"We've already taken some of the equipment to pieces a dozen times," I reminded him. "At least let two of us sleep. Let's work on a shift system or something."

Jet saw the wisdom of my suggestion. "All right," he said. "You and Mitch. Lemmy and I will carry on. We'll wake you up in four hours."

But twelve hours later we were still in exactly the same position. If there were any traceable fault it had completely escaped us.

"I don't think there's any point in going over everything again," said Jet, finally. "We'll wear out the equipment just by continually taking it to pieces."

"Then what do we do?" said Mitch. "Sit and twiddle our thumbs?"

"A rest from it will do us all good. Give us time to think. Maybe coming back fresh to the problem in another twelve hours or so might help solve it."

"In any case," I said, "we can't go on sweating our insides out. We've got to watch the oxygen supply."

"How much oxygen have we got?" asked Jet.

"At a guess," I told him, "enough for nearly twenty more days."

"Is that all?"

When we left Earth it had seemed plenty: five days' trip to the Moon, fourteen days on its surface and five days back again. Twenty-four days in all. We had brought more than we needed, of course, as a safety margin but the supply was limited. Unless we could take off within fourteen days, we wouldn't have enough oxygen left to last the journey back to Earth.

"How about food?" asked Jet.

I had that figured, too. "Normal rations would last about as long as the oxygen," I told him, "but both could be eked out over a slightly longer period if we're careful."

Jet decided to prepare for the worst. The way things were we might search the ship for a week and not find the fault. He had no intention of giving up, of course, but it was obvious that a system had to be worked out if we were to conserve the food and oxygen supply. It was decided to make thorough checks every eight hours. The rest of the time, except when food was distributed and eaten, we would lie on our bunks.

"One flashlight will remain on the control table," said Jet as he outlined the plan to us, "but it will be turned on only when needed, namely for the checks and for Doc to write his diary."

"Doc's diary," protested Mitch. "Is that so important that we have to waste valuable light on it?"

"One flashlight lasts quite a time," Jet reminded him. "Besides, now the recorder's out of action, Doc's notes will have to serve as the log. Now onto your bunks, all of you, and let's get the rota worked out for a start."

The next few days were quite the most harrowing I have ever spent. I will let my journal speak for itself:

November 12th 1965. It is now 24 days since we left Earth. 19 days since we landed on the Moon's surface, and 5 days since we tried to get off again. By now everybody, including Mitch, has resigned himself to waiting and hoping. Every few hours the radio, radar, televiewer and other installations are switched on in the hope that power has returned to the ship. So far the result has been negative. The rest of the time, except for whoever's turn it is to regulate the oxygen supply or distribute the rations, we spend lying on our bunks. The only illumination is the one flashlamp which burns over the control table. It doesn't throw much light around the cabin and most of it is in deep shadow – only the blank, expressionless faces of the dials and gauges staring dimly at us from the darkness that is the wall. The dull gleam of the metal that goes to make up the concave roof reflects what light reaches it, enabling us to make out, very faintly, the door that leads to the little pilot's cabin in the ship's nose – the cabin which Jet would have entered to pilot the ship through the Earth's atmosphere on our return journey. If we could open that door and slide back the shutters that cover the airtight window, we would see the surface of the Moon, bathed in the pale, reflected earthlight – perhaps even the Earth itself. But, as with the hatch and the airlock, we have no power to open that door, so it remains shut – immovable. The time drags. Talking would make it slip by quickly, but the quicker it passes the sooner the end, whatever it may be, will be reached. We are all outwardly calm, occasionally we moke jokes, rather feeble jokes, but the reaction to them is always very good. Every man lives in fear of the others detecting that he may be – no matter how slightly – afraid.

During the oxygen check and food distribution the flashlight was left on for one hour. This gave us the opportunity to eat and to do anything else we wished while the light was still at our disposal. I filled in my journal. Mitch and Jet read their books. Lemmy looked at the photograph of his girl or played his mouth-organ.

"Jet," said Lemmy on one occasion, "how can you read a book at a time like this?"

"What else is there to do? While the light's on I might as well take advantage of it."

Lemmy grunted. He was obviously making conversation purely for the sake of it. "It's getting perishing hot, isn't it?" he suddenly exclaimed.

"With no air conditioner working," said Mitch, "what else do you expect?"

Lemmy ignored Mitch. "If only we could open a window," he said, "if only it were possible to let in some air. I bet it's cool outside."

"Minus 270 degrees centigrade," observed Mitch, "if you can call that *cool*. You'd freeze solid the moment you put a foot outside."

Lemmy went on, half to himself. "I wonder what the boys back in Australia are thinking? If things had gone as we planned it would be only a few hours now before we'd be home. They'll be looking out for us; wondering why we didn't call them again after we said we were going to take off."

"Shut up!" said Mitch.

"What a way to end up! In a rocket ship that's supposed to reach 29,000 miles an hour but can't even raise itself a foot off the ground."

"I said, shut up!" shouted Mitch. "Do you hear?"

"Lemmy," I said quietly, "it's your turn to check the oxygen supply and give out the food."

"Oh. Yes, Doc."

"Here's the light. Take it."

"You sure you don't want to go on writing for a bit?"

"No, thank you."

"How about you, Jet? You won't be able to see to read."

"I can wait," said Jet and he put his book face down on the bunk.

Actually Lemmy's turn for inspection was not for another fifteen minutes but I thought, under the circumstances, it would do no harm to let him take it a little earlier. He walked over to the control board and called to me over his shoulder:

"Oxygen pressure 29.5."

"29.5," I repeated.

"Temperature 92 degrees." He opened the locker door and chanted quite unnecessarily: "Four flasks of fruit juice, four airtight sandwich packs."

"Give them out, Lemmy." There was a note of kindness in Jet's voice. "Then go back to your bunk and try not to talk so much."

"Yes, Jet," said Lemmy meekly.

November 13th. 6 days. We are now really missing the air conditioner. The heat is almost unbearable, the thermometer standing at over 100°. We have removed most of our clothes and live in our underwear; and we can expect it to get hotter as each hour goes by. Nobody talks very much. Each man gets up, adjusts the oxygen supply and distributes the rations as his turn comes round. Almost the only words we've heard these last 2 hours were Jet's orders when we carried out the tests on the equipment, with the usual result: nothing. Jet reads constantly. Mitch lies on his bunk gazing at the ceiling while Lemmy, who has the bunk above mine, treats us to a musical recital on his harmonica.

Music can be a great consolation and most of all to the performer. But it can have the opposite effect on an unwilling audience. Lemmy had taken to playing one tune over and over again. It was the sad, old Cockney piece, 'My Old Dutch'. He dragged out the notes to fantastic lengths, putting all the passion he could into them. It was most trying to listen to and impossible to ignore. Once or twice I almost suggested to Lemmy that he gave the thing a rest, but I knew it was probably his lifeline. Unlike Jet, Mitch or myself, he had nothing else to do. At last Mitch could stand it no longer.

"Lemmy," he shouted at the top of his voice, "cut out that row, will you?"

The music stopped abruptly.

"Blimey," was the only remark that came from Lemmy's bunk.

"Easy, Mitch," admonished Jet.

"Easy! Can *you* stand it? Haven't we got enough trouble without having that awful row going on all the time?"

"Who says it's a row?" objected Lemmy.

"Why can't you play something else for a change?"

"I don't know anything else," snapped Lemmy, untruthfully.

"Then shut up and put the thing away."

"Now hold on, Mitch. Two days ago you were only too glad to hear him play."

"Well, I'm fed up with it now."

"Put it away, Lemmy," said Jet quietly.

Lemmy, as always, obeyed him. "But I got to do something to pass the time, Jet," he protested. "Just lying here hour after hour, sweating and thinking, is enough to give you the pip. Isn't there something we can do? Test the equipment again or something."

"It's not above an hour since we tested it," replied Jet.

I decided to butt in. "Lemmy's right," I said. "Lying here in silence is the very devil. We should try to do something collective for short periods. At least it would keep our minds off things for a bit."

"How about a nice stroll outside in the earthlight?" said Mitch sarcastically.

7 days. The heat gets worse. Temperature is now way above the 100 mark. None of us has hardly a stitch of clothing on and our bunks are damp with perspiration. Monotonously the time drags by; equipment check, oxygen supply, rations – and, in between, Jet doing his utmost to keep our spirits up. We must have played every parlour game that was ever invented. We lie in the dark and fire questions at each other on general knowledge. We no longer know or care whether the answers are right. And we take turns at reciting verses. It gives us something to do and takes our minds off the inevitable climax which slowly but relentlessly approaches. For, unless life returns to the ship within the next 6 days, it must be the end of us all.

We were playing Twenty Questions.

"That's fourteen points to me," said Mitch. "Right, Lemmy, your turn."

Lemmy thought for a moment. "Er – animal," he said.

"Four legs?" asked Jet.

"No."

"Two legs?" I suggested.

"No legs."

"No legs?" Mitch queried.

"No legs and it's mineral."

"But you just said it was animal."

"It's mineral," said Lemmy desperately.

"Manufactured?"

Lemmy's voice became panicky. "And big, like a huge doughnut."

"Is it manufactured?"

"Made of metal, with a dome where the hole should be."

"Lemmy," said Jet with apprehension in his voice.

"There's a blue light flashing on and off underneath – and it's coming here."

"Lemmy!" yelled Jet, trying to bring the radio operator under control.

"It's coming, I tell you. It's right on us."

"Jet," I cried, "the televiewer. It's glowing, it must be working."

Jet swung his legs over the edge of his bunk and dropped to the floor but misjudged his fall and, as he landed, sent the flashlamp flying. As it hit the floor it went out.

There was light enough coming from the screen now for us to see each other dimly. Mitch and I were quickly out of our bunks and, joining Jet at the control table, went over to get a closer look at the picture.

"Good Lord, what on earth is it?" asked Mitch.

"It looks like it's floating, flying," said Jet, "and the light – the flashing light underneath it – just as Lemmy described."

Then whatever it was passed out of view.

"It's gone," said Jet.

"But the screen's still alive," I pointed out. "You can still see the stars and . . . oh."

Even as I spoke the picture began to fade and within a few moments we were in total darkness again.

"You *could* see the stars," said Mitch.

Jet's one thought now was for Lemmy. He groped his way over to his bunk, at the same time calling: "Lemmy, are you all right?"

"What's happened to him?" I asked.

"I don't know," Jet replied. "Try to find the flashlight."

Mitch was already on his knees; groping round the floor for it.

"I've got it, Jet", he called.

"Does it work?"

"No."

"The main lights," I said; "if the power's on, they should come on, too."

I could hear Jet climbing up the ladder towards Lemmy's bunk.

"Lemmy, can you hear me? Answer me."

Then Mitch's voice came out of the darkness. "Doc, the light switch just above the control table, can you find it?"

"Yes," I said, "I've got it." I pressed it. Nothing happened. No lights came on. The ship was dead again.

I could hear Mitch fumbling inside the locker as he groped for a second flashlight. Jet's voice was now coming from above our heads; he had obviously reached Lemmy's bunk.

"Lemmy," he said gently.

Lemmy sounded utterly miserable. "Leave me alone."

"Lemmy, did you hear? It came on again. The screen was working."

Lemmy groaned.

"Lemmy, what's happened to you? What is it?"

"I heard it," said the Cockney. "That music, I heard it again."

"You did?"

"Yes. It was going to be a horse – the one that won last year's Derby."

"What was?"

"My object. But when I started to answer the questions it all got mixed up and then that music came on and all I could think of was – well, I don't know what it was now – a kind of . . ."

"You don't have to describe it, Lemmy," said Jet. We saw it on the televiewer screen. We all saw it."

"Eh?"

"Yes, with a flashing light under it just as you described. It seemed to be flying towards us, then moved up and out of range, almost as though it might have passed right over us."

"Ah, that's better." Mitch had found a new flashlamp. "What a difference just a little light makes."

"The other one out of action, Mitch?" called Jet.

"Yes, Jet, it hit the floor pretty hard."

"Give it to Lemmy," said Jet. "I expect he can put it right. The rest of us will go round the ship. Carry out another full inspection just in case things are about to start working again."

It is now 3 days since the televiewer suddenly burst into life and the picture of the – whatever it was – appeared on it. Since then, the ship has been as dead as it ever was. The heat is now beyond description. We are using up the oxygen supply rapidly. I estimate we have barely enough to last 9 days more, and we need 5 of those days for the return journey ta Earth. So we have now only 4 days left – 4 days – if we haven't taken off by then . . .

That part of my journal was never finished, for Lemmy, who had been quiet for some hours, suddenly spoke up.

"Jet, why aren't you reading?"

"I've read that book four times now. I practically know it by heart."

"Is it a good book?"

"Yes, Lemmy, it's always been a favourite of mine."

"Then don't keep it all to yourself. Read us a bit."

"Yes, Jet," I said eagerly, "it'll be better than just lying here staring at the ceiling and thinking."

"I don't think you'd like it all that much," said Jet.

"How do we know," asked Lemmy, "until we've heard it?"

"Yes, go on, Jet," said Mitch, "read it – some of it at least. We can have another instalment next time the light's on."

"All right. If you really want me to."

"What's it called?" asked Lemmy. "Who's it by?"

"It's by H. G. Wells. It's called *The First Men in the Moon*."

"Oh." I could almost visualize the change of expression that must have come over Lemmy's face.

"Do you still want to hear it?" asked Jet quietly.

"Why not?" said Lemmy. "It might give us some clue to help us get out of this mess."

So Jet began and, as we followed the adventures of our literary predecessors, Bedford and Cavor, our own troubles were temporarily forgotten. At the end of an hour, when the time came to put the light out, we had journeyed to the Moon in Dr Cavor's gravityless ship.

During the next light session Jet read to us again. This time we learnt of Cavor's misfortunes on the Moon with the Selenites. According to Wells, the Moon supported not only life but a very advanced civilization. The two heroes of the famous novel had just been made prisoner by the Selenites when Jet declared that the time had come to put out the light and the reading would have to stop.

"Well," came Lemmy's voice from his bunk above, "that Bedford fellow certainly ran into a pack of trouble, didn't he?"

"An ingenious idea, those Selenites," I remarked.

"Thank goodness we didn't meet up with any," Lemmy went on. "If there's one thing we have proved by coming up here it is that there's no life on the Moon. None – at – all . . ."

The reason for Lemmy's hesitation was clear to us all. Down in the main hold of the ship there came a light but distinct tapping.

"What in Heaven's name is that?" I said.

"Mice," said Lemmy nervously.

The knocking continued for at least ten seconds. Then it stopped.

"It seems to be coming from outside, down near the stern," said Jet. I could sense him sitting up in his bunk, although none of us could see a thing.

"There it goes again," broke in Lemmy "on the other side this time."

It was, and just as strong; if anything a little louder. It was as though somebody were walking round the ship and tapping it to see what it was made of. Then came a new noise, as though a drill were being used. As the rotation – if it was rotation – of the drill became faster, the pitch of the sound became higher until it suddenly cut off, leaving the sounds to die away like the echo in a cavern.

"And what kind of noise is that?" said Mitch, unable to disguise the fear in his voice.

"Quiet," said Jet. The knocking suddenly began again, this time obviously going all round the ship. Then, as abruptly, it ceased.

"Mitch," said Lemmy breathlessly, "turn on the light."

It came on and we all felt better. But none of us spoke for at least an hour.

"Whatever it was," said Jet at last, "it must have gone away."

"Do you think they'll be back?" said Lemmy.

"How should I know?" said Jet irritably. "Keep quiet and listen."

13 days. The strange tapping sounds we heard 3 days ago have not been heard since. We have no idea what they were. Now there is only 1 day left. Unless we take off tomorrow, we cannot hope to reach the Earth alive. Soon, in just an hour or two, the sun will be rising over the Cape and we will have been here one full lunar day. From the Earth, the Moon will rapidly be approaching full. Hundreds of astronomers all over the world will be looking for us. We are too small to be seen but, with luck, while the sun is still low on the lunar horizon, somebody might see our long shadow and recognise it. That will tell them that we are still here. They won't be able to help us, but at least they'll know we haven't wandered off into the void of space – perhaps to spend eternity as a tiny, artificial asteroid in an orbit round the sun.

The time had come for the light to be extinguished and I closed my journal and put it away in my locker. I had hardly done so when an excited cry came from Lemmy.

"Hey, Jet, the televiewer!"

"What about it?" said Jet.

"It's come on. It's working."

Mitch, Jet and I sprang out of our bunks and onto the floor, Jet landing only an inch or two away from me. And then came a click and a whirr as the air conditioner turned itself on.

"The power," I said, "it must be back. The ship's alive again."

"The light," cried Mitch, "try the light."

That's just what Jet was doing. He pressed the switch and instantly the cabin was illuminated in what seemed to us the brightest and most comforting light we had seen in years.

"Lemmy," ordered Jet, "get to the radio. See if that's working. The rest of you get to your own controls. Check everything."

We needed no second bidding. I went over to my control board and saw that, for the first time in fourteen Earth days, the automatic oxygen supply as well as the air conditioner was now in working order. I announced the fact that we should start cooling off soon and get back to something like normal temperature. A few moments later Mitch proclaimed that the fuel gauges were working and the indications were that the tanks were full and everything was OK.

"Thank God," said Jet, "and not a day too soon."

"Radio's going," came Lemmy's voice from the control table. "Transmitter registers full aerial current."

"Then see if you can contact Earth, Lemmy, for Pete's sake."

"What do you think I'm doing?"

"Come on, Mitch," said Jet, "let's go right through the ship. One more thorough check. See if we're fit for take-off."

"I don't see why not," said Mitch. "All we needed was power and we've got it. We're going home." He began to laugh, almost hysterically. "We're going home."

Why the power should suddenly come on in this way none of us had the least idea. It was now one full lunar day and night since we had landed in the Bay, almost to the hour. Outside the ship the sun would once again be rising over Cape Laplace. It occurred to me that perhaps the lunar darkness had something to do with our power failure. It was evening when the power cut off and now that dawn was breaking outside the power had come on again. But there was no time to hold an inquest now. We had to get off the Moon and back to Earth as quickly as possible or our oxygen supply would be too low to last us the journey. I decided to discuss my theory with the others while we were coasting back home.

Meanwhile Lemmy was still trying to contact Control but without success. Mitch and Jet had completed their inspection and declared the ship ready for take-off. But we just had to be sure that Control realised we were about to do so. Failure to contact them would not prevent our taking off if we wished, but Control's help was essential if we were to be sure of making a safe landing when we reached Earth.

"I'm sorry, Jet," said Lemmy after the Captain had asked him how he was doing. "I can't get a squeak out of 'em."

"You're sure your transmitter's OK?"

"Sure I'm sure. They can't be listening up there."

"Well, you can't blame them," said Jet. "We're more than a week overdue."

"But somebody must be hearing us, somewhere. Maybe trying to contact us, too. Shall I search around the dial a bit? They're not bound to be dead on frequency."

"Yes, Lemmy, if you think it's best."

"I certainly can't do worse than I'm doing now."

Lemmy began to fiddle with the controls. We worked on ultra short wave as did many other stations on Earth and the slightest touch of the main control brought all kinds of speech and music out of the loudspeaker.

"This band seems pretty full," said Lemmy; "anybody listening to any of this should hear us, always supposing they can understand English."

We could stay on the Moon another twelve hours and still reach Earth before our oxygen supply finally gave out. But it was cutting it rather fine. And neither I, Jet nor Mitch wanted to leave it so late unless it was imperative.

"You keep right on with that radio, Lemmy. The sooner you contact Earth, the sooner we'll get away and the happier I'll be," said Mitch.

"Doing my best," came Lemmy's reply, "but nothing I've heard yet is trying to get us, that's for certain. Hullo, Earth, hullo. This is Rocketship Luna trying to contact Earth. Rocketship Luna calling from Moon. Come in please. We need to hear from you urgently."

He positioned the control to receive and listened hopefully but nothing was heard except what sounded to me like a programme of music from India or some other Eastern country. There seemed to be quite a lot of music of one kind or another.

"Music, music, music, nothing but music," said Lemmy impatiently. And then, right out of the blue, came a radio announcement that caused us all to stop whatever we were doing and listen intently. Lemmy had tuned in to London; to a news broadcast. They were announcing that there could be little hope for us or our ship. According to the announcer we had taken off from the Moon on 27th October and the last radio message Control had received from us was that we would be calling again within six minutes but that nothing further was heard. Apparently a statement from the launching ground had said that we must either have crashed back on the Moon or missed the Earth entirely, in which case we would be somewhere out in space and lost for ever. They announced our names, something about our lives, then changed the subject to a political one.

"What does that mean?" said Lemmy. "That we're dead?"

"Officially, yes," said Jet.

"Blimey. But we didn't say we had taken off, we said we were about to take off."

"Never mind," said Jet. "Get back to the transmitter and keep trying. Try to raise somebody."

There was a sudden cry from Mitch.

"Hey, Doc, Lemmy, Jet, come and take a look at this." He was standing at the control table gazing at a picture on the televiewer screen above it. In full view was the crater into which Mitch had fallen. It was slightly to one side of the ship and was completely bathed in the sunlight, although the Moon's terminator had hardly left its eastern rim. That was no more than we would have expected to see. But the astonishing thing that had brought the shout from Mitch was what was in the crater.

"Good heavens!" exclaimed Jet. "Is that what Lemmy saw during the guessing game? Is it, Lemmy? Is it?" Jet had raised his voice rather unnecessarily as though the object sitting there in the crater was Lemmy's fault.

"Well, you should know," Lemmy told him. "You said you saw it yourself. You all did."

We had, of course, but not like this, with the rising sun lighting up every detail. Before, we had only seen it as a shadow, with the pulsating light beneath it.

"That's when it must have arrived," I said, "during the guessing game. And it's been sitting out there in the crater ever since. What else are we to think?"

"Then who is it?" said Mitch. "What is it?"

"It must be H. G. Wells' lot," said Lemmy.

"There's only one way to find out," said Jet. "We'll go out there."

"Eh?" It was Lemmy again. "But we can't. It's time for us to leave. We can't spare the oxygen."

"We've got a few hours yet," said Jet.

"But you don't know what that thing is. Or what it can do to us."

"That's the very reason I want to go. This is the most important thing we've seen since we landed here. We can't pull out on it now. What would they think of us down on Earth?"

"But, Jet . . ." protested Lemmy.

"You willing to come with me, Mitch?" went on Jet, ignoring Lemmy's plea.

"I'll say," said Mitch. "I'm all for it."

"Then get the suits, Lemmy. Mitch and I are going out."

Chapter 8
WATCH YOUR STEP, EARTHMEN

The object sitting outside in the crater in which Mitch had nearly lost his life was about sixty feet in diameter and fitted the 'bowl' very snugly. It was, as Lemmy had said during the guessing game, doughnut-shaped, and covered by a semi-circular dome.

The space ship, for that is what I took it to be, rested directly on the crater floor. Its walls were perfectly smooth; there was no kind of opening. If anybody was inside this strange craft, they made no attempt to show themselves. If anybody had come out of it, they had left no tracks behind.

Before he and Mitch entered the airlock, Jet promised not to wander out of range of the televiewer and to keep in constant radio contact. They took a camera with them.

Meanwhile Lemmy was still trying to contact base. While Jet and Mitch were in the airlock he picked up something.

"Hey, Doc," he called excitedly, "I've got 'em."

"Is it Control?" I asked.

"I'm not sure. It's so faint. Listen."

I did and finally made out a weak, rather tinny voice.

"Hullo, Luna – hullo," it said.

"Blast that French station," said Lemmy as the voice was drowned out. "Hullo, Earth, Rocketship Luna calling. From the Moon. Come in – whoever you are – come in please."

"Weather Station XLG, calling from Greenland." The voice was clearer now. "Calling Rocketship Luna, and if this is a joke it's a pretty poor one."

I thought Lemmy was going to explode. "Rocketship Luna calling Weather Station XLG. And if you think it's a joke to be stranded on the Moon for fourteen days, you come and try it."

"But," came the voice, "we thought all hope for you had been abandoned."

"It will be unless somebody does something about us, and quick," snapped Lemmy.

"Who is it?" asked Jet over the intercom.

"Never mind," replied Mitch impatiently. "Let's get outside. Lemmy can handle the radio."

"OK, then, Doc," said Jet. "Open the door."

"Main door opening," I announced, and the whirr of the heavy motor filled the cabin.

"Where did you say you were, Luna?" came the faint but persistent voice from Earth.

"Where do you think?" said Lemmy. "On the Moon, of course. Been stuck up here a fortnight, Earth time, and unable to communicate due to power failure. Can you help us?"

"We're in contact with London. Will that help you?"

"I'll say it will. Tell them we're trying to contact the launching ground at Luna City, Australia. Ask London to raise them and tell them to communicate with us, and say it's urgent. Very urgent. A matter of life and death."

By now Mitch and Jet had reached the Moon's surface and were making their way towards the crater.

"I have you in full view," I told them. "Does that thing look any different now you're closer to it?"

"No, it doesn't. It still appears to be made of metal. No visible seams or doors in the sides."

"Check," I told him.

"We're going to approach it now, Doc, for a closer look."

"Watch your step."

"We will."

I had no doubt that Jet would be cautious, but I wasn't sure about Mitch. The object in the crater seemed to excite him beyond reason.

"Jet," I heard him saying, "this is the biggest thing that could have happened to us. This must mean there is life in other parts of the universe."

"Now don't let's go jumping to any hasty conclusions," said Jet firmly. "We'll just take a close look at it, get some photographs, then go back into the ship and head for home."

Meanwhile, the radio operator in Greenland came through again:

"Hullo, hullo, Rocketship Luna. Weather Station XLG calling Rocketship Luna. Over."

"Hullo, XLG," said Lemmy cheerfully, "Luna calling."

"Have passed your message to London who are now contacting Luna City. Keep listening out. You can expect to hear from them shortly."

"Thank you, Greenland, thank you very much. If you're ever in London I'll buy you a drink."

"We could do with it now; it's darned cold where we are."

"Cold!" said Lemmy. "You should come up here if you want to know what cold is. And heat too."

"Are you all safe? Jet, Mitchell and Doc Matthews?"

"Yes, thanks."

"Glad to hear it," replied the weather station. Now you'd better listen out for Luna City. They'll be calling you soon. Good luck, Luna."

"Thanks, and thanks for your help," said Lemmy.

"Hullo, Doc – Jet calling."

"Receiving you," I told him. "Go ahead."

"We're getting very close to the crater now. Keep us in range."

"Sure thing," I replied.

Then came the longed-for voice of Control.

"Hullo, Luna. Hullo, Rocketship Luna. Control calling. Can you hear me? Come in please."

Lemmy danced up and down in his excitement.

"Control, it's Control. Did you hear that, Doc? We've got 'em. Hullo, Control. Lemmy calling. Lemmy Barnet calling from the Moon. Where've you been all this time?"

"Where have you been? What happened? Why didn't you take off?"

"We couldn't. The whole ship packed in. We've been stuck up here ever since, but we're all right now."

"Well, thank goodness for that. We'd given you up as lost."

"Well, we're not. We're all here. Large as life and can't wait to . . . oh blimey! Hullo, Earth . . . hullo."

Out of the loudspeaker came the weird, almost musical sounds we had all heard before. The noise sent a cold chill down my spine.

I looked at Jet and Mitch who were now almost on the crater's rim. They were standing, rooted to the ground, watching the dome of the space ship. It was slowly opening. I fully expected something to come out. What, I hadn't a clue. A monstrous-looking, semihuman being? Octopus-shaped Martians? How was I to know? I almost trembled for the safety of Jet and Mitch standing out there, without weapons and completely unprotected against whatever might emerge from the strange object they had gone to inspect.

My first reaction was to call Jet and Mitch back. But Jet needed no bidding. He was all for making a strategic retreat, but Mitch had other ideas.

"You can go back if you want to," he said, "but I'm not going. Not yet."

"Mitch," I called, "where's your common sense? Jet, bring him back."

"Yes, come on, Mitch. I'm ordering you back to the ship."

"And I'm not going," he said.

"But Mitch . . ." went on Jet.

"You're not afraid, are you?" asked the engineer.

"Don't be absurd. But suppose there's something in there? Something hostile. How do we defend ourselves? We have no weapons – nothing."

"Even if we had they probably wouldn't be any good."

"That's all the more reason for caution," said Jet. "If we stay out here and anything happens to us, what about Lemmy and Doc? How do they get home?"

"I don't give a darn," said Mitch obstinately. "I'm going on. I'm going right up to that thing and if nothing comes out I'm going to take a look inside."

"Oh no you're not," said Jet. "It's too risky."

And with that, he took Mitch's arm and tried to pull him back.

"Jet – Mitch," I called, "for God's sake, don't struggle. The suits – you might damage them."

Mitch laughed triumphantly.

"Did you hear that? If you use force you might kill us both. Ha, that's better," he said as Jet released his hold; "fighting won't get us anywhere."

"Mitch," said Jet, "what's got into you?"

"It shouldn't be hard to figure out," said the Australian. "For years I've worked on our ship – sweating my guts out designing her and building her. And then, when we get here, there's another one. Completely different, probably holding a lot of secrets about long-distance space travel. And you want me to bypass it. Go back home without so much as taking a look at this one."

"We've photographed it, haven't we?" said Jet.

"Photographs – what can they tell us? You might as well have photographed the image on the televiewer screen."

"Mitch," said Jet resignedly, "what exactly do you want to do?"

Mitch spoke slowly and deliberately. "I want to go up to that thing. To touch it. To walk all round it and examine it."

"But the top has just opened. Something must have opened it and that something may come out."

"I'm prepared to risk it. Now do you want to come with me or not?"

Jet hesitated only a moment and then said: "All right."

"No, Jet, wait!" I called.

By this time Lemmy had given up his attempt to re-contact Control and had come over to my side.

"For heaven's sake, Jet, do as Doc says," he pleaded.

"Mitch," said Jet deliberately, "I'll come as far as the crater's rim. If you want to go down into it, you go. But don't leave my sight."

"All right," said Mitch. "It'll be better than nothing."

"Did you hear that, Doc?" asked Jet.

"Yes," I replied.

"Then keep your eye on that screen. If you see anything wrong, or anything peculiar that we don't notice, tell us at once."

"Yes, Jet."

"Then come on, Mitch," he said, "let's go. But slowly, take your time."

"Blimey, Doc," said Lemmy as we watched the two men walking round the edge of the crater to the side where the door had opened. "Why can't they leave that thing out there alone and let us go home?"

"Quiet, Lemmy," I told him, "Mitch is going down into the crater now. Hullo, Jet – everything all right?"

"Up to now it is."

"How about you, Mitch?" I asked.

"I'm not dead yet," he replied. "Walking across the crater floor now."

I could just see the top of his head as he descended the wall. Within a minute or two he was close enough to the strange craft to run his gloved hand over her.

"Hm," I heard him say, "she seems to be made of metal all right."

"What kind of metal?" asked Jet.

"Wouldn't like to say. Looks like aluminium but I don't suppose it is."

Mitch lifted his foot and gave the wall a solid kick. As he did so a hollow, metallic boom came out of the intercom speaker.

"And darned solid, too," said Mitch.

"Hey," called Jet, "do that again."

"Do what?"

"Kick it."

Mitch kicked it.

"Did you hear that?"

"Hear what?"

"Your kick. I heard it."

"Impossible," said Mitch. "You can't hear any noise up here. No atmosphere for sound waves to travel in. Besides, you've got your helmet on."

"I didn't hear it direct," said Jet, "I heard it through my radio. Doc, Lemmy, did you hear it?"

"Yes, Jet," I told him, "we did."

"Do it again, Mitch," said Jet. Mitch kicked the thing for the third time.

"Ha," he said, "heard it myself then. It definitely came through the radio."

"But how could it?" asked Lemmy.

"There's only one explanation," said Jet. "That thing itself or something inside it *is* a radio; a transmitter of some kind. It transmitted Mitch's kicks and our sets picked them up"

"Hey, Jet," said Mitch, "I'm going to walk round this thing."

"No," I begged him, "it will take you out of range of the televiewer."

"Oh, it won't take a couple of minutes," he said "I'll keep talking, so you'll know I'm still here."

"No, Mitch," said Jet.

He ignored the order. "Here I go, walking round."

"Mitch, will you listen to me?"

"Now on the western side. No different here and no way in from this side either that I can see."

Mitch was completely lost to view by this time. "Now on the southern side. Hey . . ."

"What is it?" said Jet anxiously.

"There's one thing about this ship that's the same as ours."

"What's that?" asked Jet.

"A retractable ladder, and right now the rungs are extended. It's almost like an invitation to go in."

"Never mind that," said Jet, "keep walking. Just go round."

Mitch didn't reply. The next moment his head appeared over the side of the ship near the door. Jet saw him.

"For God's sake, be careful, Mitch – what are you doing?"

"Just taking a look at things, that's all. Don't think there's anything here to be scared of. Say, I can see right down into this thing now – right down into the cabin."

Jet's curiosity overcame his caution.

"What's in there?" he said.

"Nothing," said Mitch slowly.

"Are you sure?"

"Of course I'm sure. Just a circular cabin, flat floor, plain walls and a ladder leading out of it. I'm going in."

"Oh no," said Lemmy.

We looked at each other helplessly as we heard Mitch's footsteps descending the ladder inside, echoing over our personal radios.

"Well," he said suddenly, "I'm in, and it's not so empty as I thought."

"How do you mean?" asked Jet.

"Well, the walls seem to be made of octagonal-shaped panels, and there are two rows of buttons at the top of one of them."

"Leave them alone, don't touch them."

"I'm not that crazy. Beats me where the crew can be – if it ever had a crew."

"How else could it get here?"

"Could be remote controlled."

"Yes, I suppose it could, but who by and where from?"

"Search me. Meanwhile I think I'll search this cabin. Perhaps this is just the airlock or something and the crew's quarters are further inside. Maybe under the floor."

If Mitch said anything more we didn't hear it, because at that moment everything was drowned by the space 'music' we had heard so often before. Lemmy grew more agitated than ever.

"Oh no, Doc," he said, "Listen; it's here again."

"Jet – Jet," I called. But he couldn't have heard us for he made no reply. As always when this weird music was around, parts of the ship ceased to function.

"What about Mitch inside that thing?" said Lemmy fearfully. "What's happening to him?"

I called him. "Hullo, Mitch – hullo. Can you hear me? Hullo."

But, as with Jet, I got no answer. I could see Jet standing near the crater, looking up towards the cabin of the ship. He was waving his arms as if trying to communicate something to us. Then he moved closer to the rim and slowly and carefully began to descend its wall. As suddenly as it had begun, the noise stopped.

Hoping the radio would be working again I gave Mitch another call. I got no reply but discovered that Jet at least could hear me for he, too, was now trying to contact Mitch.

"Hullo, Mitch, are you all right? Can you hear us?"

"Why on earth did he have to go in that thing?" said Lemmy.

"And why doesn't he answer us?" I asked.

"Hullo, Mitch," said Jet once again.

"Hullo, Jet, what's the panic?" Mitch replied.

"Didn't you hear us calling you?" said Jet.

"Didn't you hear that music?" put in Lemmy.

Mitch's voice sounded strange, as though he were speaking from a long distance. "It's nothing to be scared of."

"Eh?' said Lemmy.

"I said it's nothing to be scared of."

"That's what I thought you said."

"None of us is going to be hurt. This ship is just different from ours, that's all. Run on an entirely different principle."

"Mitch," said Jet, "what on earth are you talking about?"

"It's all so simple."

"Mitch, either come out of there or I'll come in myself and pull you out."

"No, Jet, don't," said Lemmy.

"That would be asking for trouble," said Mitch firmly.

"What do you mean?"

"Stay where you are. Don't attempt to move any closer."

"What's gotten into him, Jet?" I said.

"I don't know, Doc," came Jet's worried reply. "Is the recorder going?"

"Of course it is."

"Then watch it closely. Make sure you take down every word he says."

Mitch's voice continued. "This ship is from another world. Millions of miles away. Hundreds of light years. It's from the other side of the universe."

"But that's impossible," said Jet. "For anything to travel that far would take thousands of years."

"Television would seem impossible to an ancient Egyptian."

"I'm not an ancient Egyptian," said Jet angrily.

"You're right. Prehistoric man would be a better description."

"Mitch, what's the matter with you?"

"Time, that's the secret. Journeys through time. Leave here – whoosh. Next moment you pop up a thousand years from now, or back a couple of thousand."

"Mitch, for heaven's sake, what's this all about?"

"Can you explain a geometrical problem to a monkey? You'll just have to take my word for it."

"He's crackers," said Lemmy. "Whatever happened to him in there has sent him clean off his rocker."

"Mitch," said Jet firmly, "listen to me."

"No, you listen to me. What are you doing here? Where are you from?"

"Doc," Jet appealed, "what can we do?"

"Keep talking to him, Jet," I said. "Keep talking – humour him."

"Well," came Mitch's voice, "are you going to answer my question?"

"We're from the Earth," said Jet as pleasantly as he could, "but you know that."

"At first we thought you might be, then we decided you must be from some other planet."

"Huh?"

"Is that a surprise? That there are other people in the universe besides yourself?"

"Well, I suppose it's possible."

"Possible? Life is universal. It crops up wherever it's given the slightest chance. Did you think your tiny planet was unique? There are millions of stars and planetary systems. Millions of planets teeming with life."

"He must be crackers," broke in Lemmy.

"Quiet," I said, "he can hear every word you say."

"You find all this hard to believe, don't you?"

"It's not that, Mitch," said Jet, "but this is so unlike you."

"Now you're beginning to understand."

"What do you mean by that?"

"Why do you interrupt the peace of your sister planet? What is your business here?"

"Oh, surveying, photographing, the establishment of a lunar base – in time."

"Not in time, Jet. You haven't conquered that yet."

"How do you mean?" Jet sounded desperate.

"You've got a lot to learn. Already you're tearing your own planet to pieces, destroying it, and now you mean to do the same here. Isn't that your intention?"

"If there are minerals here of use to us," said Jet defensively. "I expect other men will come up from Earth and dig them out. If our civilization is to progress we need fuel, metal, radioactive materials; and the Moon appears to have great stores of them. Supplies on Earth can't last for ever."

There was a slight pause before Mitch replied.

"One day you will find that they can."

"What?" said Jet.

"Just watch your step, Earthmen. There are things out here on the fringe of space you don't comprehend, can't understand, will never understand, that no beings in a three-dimensional world can ever hope to understand."

"Three-dimensional? You mean there is another dimension?"

Mitch never replied to the last question. The music came on again and almost at once, faded out. Before I could open my mouth to call Mitch again, his voice came through the intercommunication speaker.

"I can't understand it," he said quite normally now. "I don't understand it at all."

"Hullo, Mitch. Mitch," said Jet.

"Hullo, Jet," said Mitch. "It's no good, it's beyond me."

"What is?"

"All these panels and buttons. There don't seem to be any doors, nothing. If there is a way further into this ship it's absolutely undetectable."

"Mitch," said Jet firmly, "come out of there."

"Come out?" said Mitch, "But I've only just this second got in."

"Come out? Do you hear?"

"But I can't leave now . . . Oh!"

It was the first time I had ever heard Mitch sound scared.

"What's the matter?"

"I don't know. But I'm getting out and damn quick."

"Here he comes, Jet," I said, as Mitch's head appeared through the door of the dome.

He was in such a panic that instead of going round and descending by the ladder, he risked his neck and his suit by jumping down into the crater. And then, having landed safely, began clambering up the crater's wall as fast as he could.

"Mitch, be careful," called Jet, "don't run."

He took no notice, but on reaching the rim grabbed Jet's outstretched hand and pulled himself up to ground level. We could hear Mitch's breathing as he said:

"Good Lord Jet, that thing's alive."

"Alive," said Jet, "how do you mean?"

"Well, I don't know. I can't explain. It began to vibrate."

"Is that all?"

"It's enough, isn't it?"

A movement on the televiewer screen caught my eye.

"Look, Mitch," I cried, "the door – it's closed."

"I told you, it's alive," he said grimly. "I got out just in time."

"Let's get back into Luna," said Jet, "before we all go crazy."

Less than ten minutes later they were safely inside.

"Now," said Jet, "let's get this straight. What were you talking about in that ship, Mitch?"

Mitch looked blank.

"Doc," said Jet, "you recorded everything, didn't you?"

"Sure, Jet."

"Then play it back; let Mitch hear it."

"I don't know what the hell you're talking about," said Mitch. "Is this some kind of a joke?"

"Here it comes," I told him, and as I switched on the recorder Mitch's voice came out of the loudspeaker.

"Good Lord," he exclaimed, "is that me?"

"It's your voice, isn't it?" asked Jet.

"Yes, but I never said any of those things. I wasn't in that ship long enough to say the half of that."

"But you were, Mitch. And the recorder is proof of it."

"Then let me hear it for myself."

We all listened intently as the strange conversation unfolded once more. It made no more sense to me than it had done in the first place; to Mitch neither, apparently, for as we reached the end of the piece and I switched off the machine, he passed his hand across his face in bewilderment.

"Well?" asked Jet.

"It's fantastic," said Mitch, hollowly. "It's unbelievable. What does it all mean?"

"I wish I knew," replied Jet. "But that music we've been hearing, the failure of the ship to work, and now this must all be connected in some way. It's as though whoever controls that ship has either been trying to contact us, or put us out of action."

"Contact us?" said Mitch. "You mean using me as a medium or something – oh, it's impossible. Who are *they* anyway? Where do they come from?"

"The other side of the universe," Lemmy reminded him, "according to you or, should I say, your voice."

"And the only way they could do that," said Jet slowly, "would be to travel through time. Yes," he went on, his voice filled with wonder, "that could be it – time travellers."

"Time travellers?" queried a puzzled Lemmy. "What's he talking about, Doc?"

"Well," I said, "it's been known for years that the only way to get to the really distant stars is to travel through time, but I don't see . . ."

"What was it your voice said, Mitch?" continued Jet excitedly, "You haven't conquered time yet. But they have, don't you see? They must have done."

Lemmy was completely at sea. "Then why couldn't they have arrived a hundred years from now or a hundred years ago?" he demanded. Why pick on the very time we land here?"

"And," I pointed out, "even if we accept that theory, why should they try to scare us off and put our ship out of action?"

"Maybe they were as surprised to see us as we were to see them. Maybe just as scared, too."

"Eh?" interrupted Lemmy, "them afraid of us?"

"Why not?" asked Jet.

"Look," said Lemmy very puzzled, "if they can travel through time, whatever that means, they must be vastly superior to us in every way."

"Lemmy," asked Jet, "can you fly and find your own way home instinctively, like a homing pigeon?"

"Do I look as though I can?" retorted Lemmy.

"Well then," said Jet, "do you consider the homing pigeon superior to you? More intelligent? Just because he can do something you can't?"

"No, I don't," said Lemmy emphatically.

"Well, that's how it might be. Perhaps whoever made that ship out there can travel in time, not because they are necessarily superior to us, but because that's the natural way for them to travel. Maybe they couldn't travel through space if they tried."

"Yes," said Lemmy slowly, "I see what you mean – I think."

"If only we had their secret," said Mitch. "Think of the things we could do."

"If only we had the oxygen," said Lemmy, "think of the time we could stay here. Aren't we ever going home?

"Lemmy's got something there," I said. "Maybe we've stumbled up against something that's going to rock modern thought to its very foundations. But unless we get word of it back to Earth, and quick, it's going to be lost for ever."

"Lemmy," ordered Jet, "open up the radio. Call Earth, tell them we'll be leaving in a few minutes, tell them we're coming home."

"That's the best bit of news I've heard up to now," said Lemmy, already halfway towards the control table.

"Doc, Mitch," went on Jet, "start getting ready. Take-off in thirty minutes."

Mitch and I set to, trying to forget our strange experience and to concentrate on the job in hand. We were going home. But our business with the Moon wasn't quite finished. The last thing we were scheduled to do before we finally headed for Earth was to encircle the Moon once and take a look at the other side – the side no man on Earth has ever seen. In Luna such a trip was a simple matter. The method was to take off, climb a few miles, turn the ship at the necessary angle until it was flying parallel with the Moon's surface, and then continue round the globe in free orbit until our nose was again pointing towards the Earth. Then the motors would be cut in, our course changed from a circular to a straight one and the long coast back to home would begin.

We strapped ourselves into our bunks and prepared to fire the motors. Before leaving, the television camera in the ship's nose was rotated for one last look at the lunar landscape. The ship, or whatever it was, had gone. The crater was empty. Five minutes later we were on our way.

The orbit we entered was about a hundred miles above the Moon's surface, close enough to give us a good view and to enable us to take sharp photographs of the principal features as they passed below. I was to handle the camera while Mitch and Jet observed the Moon through the televiewers.

At first sight, the far side was very little different from the Earth side. There were the same mountains, craters and plains.

"Hey, Jet," Mitch called suddenly from his position at the control table. "Come over here, look at this."

"What is it, Mitch?"

"Directly below us now. One of the biggest craters I've ever seen, about twice the size of Copernicus. But it's full of little craters, tiny ones in regular lines."

I took a look for myself through the telescopic viewfinder of the camera. It was just as Mitch said. Such formations on the Moon are not an uncommon sight. Many of the larger craters, in fact, seem to form themselves into fairly straight lines, but the unusual thing about the domes we were now seeing was the pattern they made; it was perfectly symmetrical. There were twenty of them altogether in four lines of five.

Jet was very puzzled. "There is a tendency for craters on the Earth side to form lines of a sort," he said, "but not like this. This doesn't look natural."

"It isn't," said Lemmy positively. "Those craters are moving."

"What?" said Jet, in alarm.

"Yes," I confirmed. "They're moving all right. They're leaving the ground."

"Good Lord," exclaimed Jet, "they're not craters at all. They're ships, just like the one that landed near us."

"And they're coming up here," said Lemmy unhappily.

One by one the objects down below were taking off and climbing upwards. We were, of course, moving extremely rapidly and soon left the crater way behind us. But to keep it and the strange objects in view, Jet ordered Lemmy to switch on the stern view camera. We could now see the space ships hovering behind and below us. Soon, drawn up in a circular formation, they had risen to our level and were advancing relentlessly. We stared, horrified and yet fascinated. There was no doubt now. It was us they were after.

"Isn't there something we can do?" broke out Lemmy. "Turn on the motor – get away from them – something?" His voice rose sharply.

"No," said Jet firmly. "Not yet. If we turn on the motor now we'd go shooting off into space and might miss the Earth altogether. We've got to wait till our nose is pointing towards home."

"They're keeping their distance at the moment anyway," I said, as much to reassure myself as Lemmy.

"Good God! Look at that!" exclaimed Mitch. The circular formation had broken up, leaving only one of the craft flying on a steady course. The rest were weaving about it, like fighter aircraft attacking a bomber. "I'd give five years of my life to know how they manoeuvre like that, in space."

"I'd give ten to know how to get away from them," said Lemmy.

"Photograph them, Doc," said Jet urgently. "Get as many pictures as you can."

"Sure," I told him. It was a relief to have something to do. Almost as though they had heard Jet's order, the strange ships ceased their acrobatic gyrations and drew up in a crescent formation, the horns pointing towards us.

"This is it," said Lemmy. "They're closing in for the kill."

The ships were indeed, approaching rapidly, and we could now see that they were in every way identical with the one Mitch had entered before we took off.

"And we haven't even got a gun," protested Lemmy.

"Doubt if it would do much good if we had," said Jet, "the way these things manoeuvre. All we can do is carry on as we intended. Stand by to set course."

Two minutes later we had climbed onto our couches and switched on the motor. Pressure rapidly increased and our velocity rose from 3,500 miles an hour to 5,600. At that speed, our nose pointed directly to Earth, the motor was cut and the pressure ceased.

"Earth dead centre," said Mitch, "Course correct."

"Ships still following," said Lemmy "and getting closer."

Although we had known it to be highly unlikely, I think we had all half hoped that our burst of speed might have shaken off our pursuers. Now there was nothing more we could do. We were at their mercy. Automatically we left our bunks and went round checking the dials and gauges. Everything was in good order. We could be reasonably sure of making a safe landing on Earth – if we were allowed to get that far.

"Call up Control, Lemmy," said Jet, "tell them we've circled the Moon and are on course for home."

"Hardly seems worth while," said Lemmy staring at the televiewer. The ships were gaining on us at tremendous speed.

"Call them up, Lemmy, do you hear?" shouted Jet angrily.

Without further comment, Lemmy went over to the radio panel, made his preliminary call and then switched the radio to "Receive" position. Instead of the friendly, comforting voice of Control we heard, much louder and stronger than ever before, the eerie sounds that had dogged us ever since take-off. There was no longer any doubt that the music was in some way connected with the craft now close behind us. The leading ship on the left side peeled off and approached us so fast that it filled the whole screen before sailing out of sight over our heads, causing us all to duck instinctively. Almost immediately came a second and a third and a fourth. They were either attacking us or trying to scare the daylights out of us.

Suddenly Jet turned to me and said: "Do you feel anything?"

"Gravity is returning to the ship."

"Impossible," said Mitch.

"It is, I tell you."

"He's right, Mitch," I said, "I can feel it, too."

It was getting strong, very strong. Our speed was increasing, extremely rapidly, and by now the pressure was so great it was becoming difficult to stand up.

"Back to your couches," shouted Jet. "Everybody get on your couches. Lie flat."

We all made the effort, but it was hopeless. The pressure was so great it was impossible to walk. My knees gave way and I hit the floor. From where I lay I saw Mitch go down on his knees and then roll over as he tried to turn onto his back. I heard a groan from Lemmy as he went down, banging his head on the side of the control table as he fell.

All the discomforts of the take-off were on us again, only this time there was no soft couch to lie on, nothing but our thin crew suits between us and the hard metal floor. The pain was agonising.

Just as I felt I could stand it no longer, the cabin roof at which I was gazing became blurred. Then I lost consciousness.

Chapter 9
LOST IN SPACE

I awoke as from a nightmare. I had been in a torture
chamber, strapped to the floor, and the ceiling had
gradually descended to crush me out of existence. My body
ached in every limb. I had a violent headache and a dreadful
feeling of nausea. Then I came to, to find Jet bending over me.

"How do you feel, Doc?" he was saying.

"Dreadful," I told him. "What happened?"

"I don't know."

"How do *you* feel?"

"Same as you. Awful. But the pressure's gone now."

"Did you black out?" I asked him.

"Yes – we all did."

"How about Mitch and Lemmy?"

"They're still unconscious, flat out. Do you think you can
get up?"

I tried. It was difficult and rather painful, but I made it.
Lemmy was lying near the control table, a nasty bump
showing on his forehead and a trickle of blood down the side
of his face. Mitch was not far from his bunk which he had tried
to reach before the increasing pressure overtook him and
pinned him to the floor.

Lemmy moaned. We went over to him. After a few
moments he opened his eyes.

"You all right, Lemmy?" asked Jet.

He looked up at us in a daze. "Oh," he groaned, "leave me
alone. I feel shocking."

Mitch stirred. A cursory examination showed he was in a bad way, far worse than when we had first taken off from Earth and he had suffered so badly from space sickness. He didn't reply to any of my questions; all he could manage was a faint noise at the back of his throat.

"Jet, give me a hand, will you?" I called.

Jet left Lemmy at once and between us we lifted the Australian onto his bunk. When we had finished it suddenly occurred to me that I should not have needed Jet's help, for under gravityless conditions Mitch should have weighed nothing.

"We must still be accelerating," Jet said. "Not very much but enough to give us something like the strength of gravity we know on Earth. Come on, Doc. Let's see if we can find out what's happened to us. We'll take a look outside first. See if those ships are still there."

Jet switched on the televiewer. The screen glowed, and hundreds of bright white lines ran down the frame from top to bottom. I thought at first that it wasn't quite in focus, but no matter how much Jet fiddled with the controls the lines remained.

"It's crazy – the tube must have gone," he said.

"No, Jet, I don't think it's that."

"Then what is it? Why don't we get a clear picture?"

"It is a clear picture," I told him.

"Huh?"

"Those bright streaks are points of light travelling from the top of the frame to the bottom. They're stars."

"Stars?"

"Yes, Jet. Don't you see? The ship is spinning, turning head over heels, and those lines are the stars flashing by as we turn. That's why we can still feel a gravitational pull. It's not gravity at all, really – it's centrifugal force."

Jet gasped. "You're right, Doc. But what set us spinning?"

"I don't know, but we've got to steady her somehow – get her back on an even keel."

Jet went over to the engineering control panel and switched in the gyro. Two hours later our gyrations had ceased and once more the stars appeared on the screen as pin-points of light. We rotated the camera, hoping it would enable us to get our bearings.

"Let's look at the Moon first," said Jet, "and see exactly where that is."

In a slow sweep we searched the port side, but she wasn't there. Then we searched the starboard side and still couldn't find her. We explored the region in the stern of the ship and we explored forward, but not a sign of the Moon could we see.

"This is ridiculous," said Jet. "It must be out there somewhere."

"It should be," I told him, "but it's not. And come to that neither is the Earth nor the Sun."

"What?" exclaimed Jet.

"Well," I asked him, hoping my voice was steady, "did you see them just now?"

"No, I didn't," he said slowly.

We searched the void again but the Earth and her satellite, not to mention the Sun, had vanished from the heavens. We rotated the camera a third and fourth time, but all we saw were stars, millions and millions of stars.

Meanwhile Lemmy had got up and was trying to contact Control, but not a thing could be picked up on the receiver, no music, no speech, no sound of any kind.

"It's like every transmitter back on Earth has packed in," said Lemmy. "I can't raise a sausage – nothing – not on any band."

"Don't be ridiculous," said Jet. "Keep trying."

"Well," said Lemmy wearily, "if you say so."

For my part I had just completed the fifth full rotation of the televiewer camera with still no sign of Earth, Sun or Moon.

"But this is fantastic," said Jet. "We couldn't possibly miss objects their size. The Moon's image alone should more than fill the whole screen. We can't be that far away from it."

"We've got to face it, Jet," I told him. "They're not there, or, if they are, we can't pick them up."

"Something *must* be wrong with the televiewer," he said decisively.

"Then why do we see the stars?" I asked him.

"The only other explanation," he said, after a few seconds' deliberation, "is that we're off course."

Off course would be putting it mildly. We would have to be thousands and thousands of miles off course for this to happen. So far off course that the Moon, the Sun and the Earth, if they were there at all, would appear no larger than dots on our screen.

Jet would not trust the televiewer. He was still convinced that something was wrong either with it or the camera. I prayed that he might be right.

"The only way to prove it," he said, "is to go outside and look. Are you willing to come with me, Doc?"

I was. We put on our suits.

Lemmy left the radio to operate the airlock and five minutes later Jet and I had passed through the main door and were working our way along the hull. We anchored our safety lines to the rings near the door and walked up to the ship's nose.

It was my first experience outside while the ship was in actual flight and, for a moment, the grandeur of it drove all other considerations out of my head. We were completely surrounded by a black void. Millions upon millions of fiery spots of coloured light dotted the sky in every direction. But we could see no sign of the Sun, the Earth or the Moon. We comforted each other with the thought that perhaps we were on the wrong side of the ship and that if we went 'down under', as Lemmy described it, we would see what we were looking for from there. We went, but with the same result; nothing but stars. There was no doubt about it: somehow we had been knocked completely out of the solar system and were now travelling through the void of space, heaven knew where or in what direction.

"I can't believe it," said Jet in a hushed voice. "It's too incredible to grasp. Let's get back in the ship, Doc," he said brusquely. "The whole thing must be an hallucination. Either that or I'm having a bad dream."

"If you are," I told him, "I'm sharing it with you. No, Jet, I'm afraid we're not dreaming, not by a long sight."

We returned to the cabin to find that Mitch had now regained consciousness but was still feeling very 'crook' as he described it. We gathered round his bunk to break the news to him and to Lemmy.

"And that's the position, gentlemen," Jet told them a few minutes later. "There's no sign of the Moon, the Sun, the Earth, Mars or any of the other planets. In fact, there's no sign of the solar system at all."

"But," objected Lemmy, who had not yet grasped the full implications of what Jet had told him, "unless we find the Earth we're done for. And it shouldn't be too difficult to find," he added. "One of those stars out there must be our Sun."

"Oh sure, but how do we find out which?" I asked.

"Well," he said thoughtfully, "by the constellations. Yeah, that's it. All we've got to do is identify a few star groups, deduce our position from them and then . . ."

"Not a hope," broke in Jet. "Look at the screen. See the stars drifting by? Thousands of them. Can you pick any given constellation out of that lot?"

"*I* can't," said Lemmy, "but I'm only the radio operator."

"I'm afraid I can't either," said Jet gently. "We'll never find our way home that way."

"And the constellations as seen from here," I broke in, "right among them, as it were, look very different from what they do on Earth – unrecognisable."

Mitch had recovered sufficiently to take an active part in the discussion. "Even if we do get our bearings," he said, "how do we take the ship out of the course she's in and put her on the right one? At the speed we're travelling, I don't think cutting in the motor would make any difference."

"You mean we haven't a chance?" asked Lemmy. "No hope at all?"

"Not of getting back home," said Jet.

"But how did this happen?" asked Lemmy pathetically. "What caused it? Less than an hour ago we were quietly coasting above the Moon's surface, minding our own business, and now look at the mess were in."

"Lemmy," said Jet kindly, "none of us knows how this happened. All we can be sure of is that those ships had something to do with it. Somehow they must have increased our speed, and carried us faster and farther than man has ever dreamed he could go."

"Then where are those perishing ships?" Lemmy demanded angrily. "Why don't they show themselves? Where do you think they're taking us?"

"We don't know that they're taking us anywhere."

"Here, wait a minute," said Lemmy, as a thought struck him. "They said they came from the other side of the universe, didn't they? Maybe that's where we're going."

"You mean," asked Mitch, "that in one go they've swept us right out of our solar system and smack into the middle of eternity?"

"Yes," said Lemmy.

"Whatever that may be," I murmured.

"But we must be going somewhere," he insisted.

"Lemmy," said Jet, "the universe is vast. It's on the cards that we'll never land up anywhere."

"Eh?"

"I mean it."

"But that's impossible. Look at all those stars out there. Even if we just go drifting aimlessly on we're bound to meet up with one of them in the end."

"Every one of those stars is a million times bigger than this ship. They have been drifting out there in space for millions upon millions of years, and in all that time only an infinitesimal number have ever actually collided. So what are our chances?"

"*Millions* of years?" asked Lemmy.

"Yes," said Jet.

"How much oxygen have we got?"

"Enough for little more than four and a half days," I told him. There was a pause.

"Silly, isn't it?"

"You could look at it that way," I said.

"Those – things," Lemmy went on, "those ships or whatever they are, told us, through Mitch, that there were thousands of planetary systems in the universe, all teeming with life."

"There probably are."

"Well, if we can leave our own in such a hurry, aren't we liable to meet up with another just as quick, maybe the very one those ships come from themselves?"

"We might at that," said Jet thoughtfully. "We might do anything. We just don't know. All we do know is that we are somewhere out in space, zooming through the Milky Way at a speed probably as fast as that of light."

"And even if we did come across another – solar system," I said, "what are the chances of its planets being suitable for us to land on and, assuming they are, of our being able to survive on them?"

"Not great," said Mitch.

In our own solar system, only the Earth, so far as modern knowledge can ascertain, is capable of supporting life as we know it. Mercury is so close to the Sun that, on that planet, lead would be kept in a molten state. Venus, also, is far too hot to be comfortable and, in any case, her atmosphere contains insufficient oxygen to support any kind of life. Mars? Well, his case is, perhaps, an open question; but even there the atmosphere is so thin and oxygen content so low that the chance of anything existing other than primitive plant life is extremely remote. Life on Jupiter, Saturn or any of the far distant planets would be frozen out of existence. If, of all the planets revolving round the Sun, only the Earth is blessed with life, what chance was there of finding it among the planets of any other solar system?

For us to remain alive on another planet, it would have to resemble the Earth very closely – to have reached the same point in its life cycle. The chances were that it would not. Assuming that we were lucky enough to run up against another solar system and that we passed close enough to one of its planets to attempt a landing, we would almost certainly find it to be either in its early molten state or so far advanced as to be a barren, dead world, like the Moon. Its atmosphere could be poisonous to us – it might have no atmosphere at all. It could be so large, and its gravitational pull so great that we couldn't even stand up – or so small that we would jump fifty feet in the air at every step. It could be waterless – or entirely covered with water. There is no end to the varied conditions, and combination of conditions; there was no chance at all of finding the right one.

Lemmy looked at his feet. "Not very encouraging, is it?" he said slowly.

"I'm afraid we've all got to face up to it," said Jet firmly. "We're helpless, absolutely helpless. No idea where we are or what direction we are travelling in and, even if we knew, powerless to exert any kind of control whatever over the ship."

"I'd sit down and make out my will," said Lemmy, "but there'd be nobody to read it."

"To think that our attempt to conquer such a small part of the universe should have resulted in this," said Jet. "An endless journey through eternity."

"That's what comes of meddling with things we don't understand," said Lemmy. "We should have stayed at home, where life was worth living."

"There's no use in crying over it now," Jet replied. "We'll have to do something if only to keep our reason."

"Well, you're the captain," said Mitch. "Anything you say."

Jet took a deep breath. "For a start we'll carry out normal routine, check the equipment, call up base on the radio."

"What good will that do?" said Lemmy disconsolately. "According to you there's no radio wave could leave Earth fast enough to catch up with us."

"Even so there's no sense in sitting back and brooding over our position. We'll carry on until we . . . until . . . Lemmy, get to that radio."

"Yes, Jet."

"Mitch, as soon as you feel well enough, check the motor, fuel gauges, everything."

"Right," said Mitch.

"I'll check the radar and keep televiewer watch for the next hour. Doc."

"Yes, Jet?"

"You'll keep a log, just as you did during the long wait on the Moon. Now get started, all of you."

Lemmy went back to his radio, Jet took the televiewer and Mitch, still feeling very groggy, got slowly off his bunk and walked, rather awkwardly towards the engineering panel. I sat down at the side of the control table next to Lemmy and took out my pencil.

November 20th, 1965, Earth time [I wrote]. *It is now more than two hours since we found ourselves in these new and frightening circumstances. How we got there, what really caused it, we shall never know. The fact remains we are somewhere within the galaxy of which the Sun is a member. We deduce this from the fact that innumerable stars are constantly visible on the screen. We are like a ship at sea, drifting, only our chance of ever making land at all must be negligible. For we are adrift in space, maybe destined to wander round the universe for ever, helplessly, hopelessly, a tiny speck of humanity lost in a vast, hostile nothingness. Everybody goes about his normal duties as though we were coasting back from the Moon towards Earth and home, as indeed, but for this fantastic, stupendous trick of fate, we would be. Mitch periodically checks the motor, fuel tanks, oxygen supply and air-conditioner. Lemmy stays at the radio, trying and hoping to get some kind of contact with somebody, somehow. Jet remains at the televiewer, transfixed, hoping that, in spite of everything, something will appear on it to give us some hope, a straw to clutch.*

I was distributing food rations when Jet, who was still at the televiewer, excitedly called to all of us to join him in front of the screen. There, almost filling the frame, was a globe, shining brightly in the reflected light of its parent sun. I was so surprised I could hardly believe my eyes.

"When did you pick that up?" I asked him.

"Just a moment ago," he said. "Last time I passed this position there was nothing, but when I rotated this time, there it was as large as life."

"How did we come to miss it before?" I asked.

"I don't know, Doc," said Jet.

"It wouldn't be the Moon, would it?" suggested Lemmy hopefully.

"If it was," said Jet, "we'd probably see the Earth, too."

"Do you think we're going to hit it?"

"Unless we take some action to avoid it. Get over to the radar, Doc. See if you can calculate our speed of approach."

"Yes, Jet." I set to work. As I took the readings I could hear Mitch, Jet and Lemmy discussing the object on the screen.

"It has an atmosphere," Mitch was saying, "no doubt about that."

"Yes," said Jet, "but what is it composed of?"

"But it is a planet," I said, "an island in a limitless ocean, and we're heading straight for it. It's a chance in a million, our only hope."

"You mean we should attempt a landing on it?" asked Lemmy.

"Why not?" agreed Jet. "If we're going to die anyway, it might as well be on that, whatever it is, as out here in nothing."

"But," protested Lemmy, "we have no idea what's on it, who's on it. Think what you're doing."

"We haven't much time to think. An hour and we'll either have crashed into it or passed it by, then it will be too late."

"Well, I'm all for taking the chance," said Mitch. "Let's try to land."

"Right," said Jet. "Procedure will be the same as it would have been for landing on Earth." And with that he climbed into the pilot's compartment, put on his helmet, tested the intercom system and made ready to steer the ship through the planet's atmosphere.

"Lemmy," he said, "stay with the televiewer, will you? If you notice anything odd about that planet as we get nearer, give a yell."

"What else?" replied Lemmy, laconically.

We were now so close to the globe that half of it filled the screen.

"Jet," called Lemmy, after looking intently at the picture for a few moments, "there's a kind of bright reflection at the top of the globe, like custard over a Christmas pudding."

"An ice cap," came back Jet's voice. "Like the North and South poles of the Earth, but bigger, much bigger."

"Then we can't land there, can we?"

"No, but nearer the equator it will be warmer."

"Seem to be a lot of cloud areas," said Mitch, "and thick, too."

"All to the good," said Jet. "At least that indicates there's moisture down there."

"Water?" asked Lemmy.

"I hope so. If it isn't . . ." he broke off. "All right, Doc," he called. "As soon as you have anything worked out, let me have it, will you?"

"Right," I told him. "Won't be long now."

With Mitch's help, our velocity and height were eventually calculated. So far as we could tell, we were about 17,000 miles above the surface of the planet and our speed was approaching 10,000 mph. This, strangely, was exactly what our height and speed would have been if we had been approaching the Earth after taking off from the Moon. We passed the information on to Jet and waited for further orders.

After a minute or so Lemmy had fresh ideas as to the identity of the planet. "I suppose this couldn't be the Earth, could it?" he asked, somewhat diffidently.

"How could it," said Mitch, irritably.

"It's got land, water, clouds and ice caps."

"It isn't the Earth," said Mitch, "that's certain."

"From here it looks as though our best bet for landing will be to treat it as though it were," came Jet's voice. "Get to your posts and stand by for landing procedure."

Less than two hours later we were gliding through the upper layers of the atmosphere of this strange planet. Suddenly there came an exclamation from up in the pilot's cabin.

"What is it, Jet?" I asked.

"The wings," he came back, "they're red hot. We must have entered the atmosphere at at least 15,000 mph and we can't be doing much less than that now."

"Estimated height, 50 miles; speed, 14,500," confirmed Mitch from the control table.

"Right," said Jet, "I'll hold her to 50 miles for as long as I can. The atmosphere's resistance will slow us down and with luck we'll make a safe landing. At least we're the right way up and on a steady course."

We were now heading across the pole. Fortunately we were going too fast to have to consider landing on the ice, and we estimated that we would be well on our way towards the equator before we were anywhere near slow enough to touch down.

"You'd better convert the couches to sitting position, ordered Jet. "As soon as you've done that, train the televiewer on the surface directly below. Then between us we can select a good landing place – if there is one."

By the time we had left the ice behind, our estimated height was only 20 miles and our speed 750 mph. We were now passing over the sea. After a few minutes there came another shout from Jet.

"I can see land now," he said, "way on ahead and slightly to port. I'm going to turn and head towards it."

Lemmy and I kept our eyes glued to the televiewer screen.

"Height, 25,000 feet," said Mitch, "speed 180 miles per hour."

"Check," said Jet.

Soon the land came into view. It was mountainous.

"Blimey," said Lemmy "doesn't look very friendly, does it? About as good a spot for landing as the Swiss alps. Wonder if it's all like this – a planet of mountains?"

"Do you see any end to them, Jet?" asked Mitch.

"No," said Jet slowly, "I don't. They stretch clear to the horizon."

"Blast!"

"Some of those mountains must be 20,000 feet high at least," said Lemmy in alarm. "We'll hit 'em for sure unless we cut in the motor and rise again."

"It may come to that yet," said Jet.

"But it would be such a waste of fuel," protested Mitch.

"So what difference does it make?" argued Lemmy. "We're never going to take off again anyway. Once we've landed, we're stuck here for ever. There's nowhere else to go."

We continued our glide in silence. There was nothing but rocks and mountains, not even a tree.

"Perhaps," said Lemmy, "trees don't even grow here. Perhaps nothing grows here."

Suddenly Jet announced that he thought we were coming to the end of the mountain range. Valleys were becoming deeper and the lower slopes of some of them had a greenish tinge.

"Is it grass, Doc?" asked Lemmy.

"I wouldn't like to say from this height."

"Could be a kind of moss or lichen," suggested Mitch.

"Is that good?" asked Lemmy.

"Well, it shows *some* kind of life can exist here," I said.

"It does?"

"But it may be the only life. We were told to expect lichen even on the Moon."

"Oh."

"But these mountains are high, Doc," put in Mitch. "That's about the only kind of life that could survive on them. Maybe there are more advanced forms lower down."

"Always supposing there is a lower down," said Lemmy. "If you ask me, this planet is nothing but mountains and sea."

But Lemmy was wrong, as Jet's excited voice told us less than a minute later.

"Hey, Mitch, Doc, Lemmy," he called, "there's a great stretch of flat country ahead."

"What does it look like?" I enquired.

"I can only see it in little patches," replied Jet. "It's covered by cloud, stacks of it."

"Then what makes you so sure the country under there is flat?" Lemmy wanted to know.

"If it wasn't, I'd see the mountains jutting up through the cloud. If there's anywhere we can land, I think it's there."

"Well, if there's any chance," said Mitch, "so far as I'm concerned, the sooner the better."

"Right," said Jet; "here we go."

Soon the country that Jet had been describing was in full view on the televiewer screen. It was level all right, and we could easily have made a landing if the whole area had not been covered with forest. But Jet had not given up yet. Visibility wasn't all that good and the cloud was thicker and lower than he'd expected, but he thought he could keep under it without hitting the ground. Our height was 1,000 feet; our speed, 90 mph. We waited, over-optimistically perhaps, for Jet's next report.

"It's no good," he said, "nothing but trees. We'll have to rise again. Get above this cloud and find somewhere else."

Mitch was preparing to cut in the motor when Jet shouted, "Wait, hold on a minute. There's a gap way ahead, like a great area of the forest has been cleared – and cultivated."

"What?" I asked incredulously.

"It's true, Doc, and there's a river in front of us, running at right angles to our line of flight."

"Can you see a place to land?" said Mitch impatiently.

"And now it's raining," Jet went on cheerfully, "absolutely teeming down."

"Oh, blimey!" said Lemmy.

Mitch repeated his question.

"Yes, there are plenty of places," said Jet, "but we're going too fast at the moment. I'll have to circle and keep circling until we've slowed down."

Slowly but surely we descended. Soon our speed was only 70 mph and Jet was straightening up ready for the run in. By now it was raining bucketfuls and visibility was almost down to zero.

"Take it easy," advised Mitch. "We don't want to hit anything, not at this stage."

"Running in now," came back the pilot's reply.

Height was 500 feet.

"You'd better brace yourselves," Jet warned. "Get into your chairs." Jet now began to read off his altimeter to us. "300 – 200 – 100 – nearly there. Stand by." A pause, then: "Here it comes." Jet put the nose of the gliding rocket down to increase speed a little, then pulled back the stick, and eased her up slightly in the hope of making a pancake landing. But the undercarriage which had been put out when we first began to descend struck the ground too hard. There was a crump, a lurch, and we bounced off again. Jet apologised and told us to get ready for the second try.

"Touching down – now."

There was a jolt as we hit the ground, the ship rolled for a few yards, then jolted again as the fore-wheel made contact with the surface. At the point of impact, we must have been travelling at only 50 mph, but in spite of this I was thrown forward in my chair, the safety straps cutting into my stomach rather painfully. Then the ship shuddered to a standstill and we were down, safe and in one piece.

"Well, we've made it," said Lemmy. "We're here."

"Yes," I told him. "Heaven knows where we are, but we're here."

Chapter 10
JOURNEY THROUGH TIME

"You all right back there?" came Jet's voice. "Sorry for the bump but it was no concrete runway we landed on."

"We're fine, Jet," said Mitch, who was undoing his safety strap, "and I'm coming up to the cabin to take a look out."

"Come on then," said Jet, "not that you can see much in all this rain."

To get to the pilot's cabin now we had to go forward, for what had been one wall of our cabin was now the roof, and the roof a wall. It was certainly raining, raining as heavily as in a tropical monsoon.

"Strewth," said Lemmy, "d'you suppose it always rains like this here?"

"How should I know?" said Jet, "I'm a stranger in these parts."

"Well," I said, "it only goes to prove that life on other planets must be fundamentally the same as on Earth – green vegetation, the river, clouds, rain."

"Just like home, isn't it?" said Lemmy with forced cheerfulness, "only much wetter."

"I wonder if there's any kind of animal life?" asked Jet.

"There must be," said Mitch. "Those plots of vegetation are too regular, too uniform to grow that way naturally."

"Are you suggesting some kind of animal planted them?" queried Jet.

"Well, if they did," I said, "where are they? Where are their houses – their cities, if they have any?"

"Maybe," conjectured Lemmy, "their homes are miles from here and they travel by boat along the river."

"A good guess," said Jet, "but wide of the mark I'm sure."

"Only trying to help."

"Do you think that stuff out there is good to eat?" I asked. "Our food isn't going to last forever."

"Nor our drink," said Lemmy. "Can we drink that water or will it poison us?"

"Can we breathe the air?" said Mitch. "Is it air?"

"It may not even be safe to step outside the ship," said Lemmy slowly.

"Gentleman," said Jet, "I don't know where we are, what planet this is we've landed on, or in what part of the universe it is located, but the fact remains it looks as though we're to be here till the end of our days, and if we remain in the ship, our days are numbered at less than five."

"And if we step outside," said Lemmy, "we may not live five minutes."

"But if there *is* air out there," I suggested, "and food and water . . ."

Mitch interrupted me. "Someone will have to go out there and try it," he said.

"Go out?" said Lemmy. "Isn't there some other way?"

"What?"

"But whoever goes . . ." Lemmy paused, thought for a moment and then went on: "No, there's no other way that I can think of."

"We'll draw lots for it," said Jet.

"And how will we get out?" I asked.

"Through the airlock."

"But the moment we open the main door, whatever atmosphere is out there will rush in and fill up the vacuum. And the next time we use the airlock it will enter the ship and, if it's poisonous . . ."

"If it is poisonous," broke in Mitch, "we won't be using the airlock again anyway. Whoever's left in won't be wanting to go out."

"I'm not so sure about that," said Lemmy. "I think I'd rather be poisoned out there and get it over with than die of suffocation in here."

"All right," said Jet. "Let's get back into the main cabin, We'll draw lots."

The task fell to Lemmy. "First time I've won a draw in my life," he said, "and it has to be this." Immediately Jet volunteered to take his place but the radio operator wouldn't hear of it.

Lemmy put on his space suit, we opened up the hatch and he descended into the airlock below. The hatch was then closed and the air exhausted.

"All right, Doc," said Lemmy, "open the door and let's get out of here."

"Take it easy," said Jet to me. "Just ease the main door enough to break the vacuum. Let that air or whatever it is out there come in as slowly as possible."

"Yes, Jet," I said. "Main door opening."

"Standing by," said Lemmy.

"How do you feel?" asked Jet anxiously.

"Lonely," came the small, metallic voice.

The pressure reached maximum.

"Hey!" said Lemmy. "My suit – it's gone all flabby."

"It will," said Jet. "As the air or whatever it is comes in from outside, it will equalise the pressure."

"It'll be a lot easier to move anyway," said the Cockney.

"She must be full now," said Mitch.

Lemmy heard him. "Then open the door properly," he said. "Let me get out there and get this over with."

I opened it, then pressed the button which operated the small ladder leading from the main door down to the ground. We couldn't see Lemmy now, of course, but we heard him describing his progress.

141

"Here I go," he said. "I'll go round to the front so you can all see me through the pilot's window." Soon he was making his way through the wet grass.

"How is it to walk?" asked Mitch.

"It's not walking that worries me, it's how long I'm going to be able to. Now going round to the nose of the ship."

We moved over to the pilot's cabin and crowded into the tiny compartment.

"Hullo, Lemmy," Jet told him, "we can see you now. You all right?"

"I'll tell you in just a few minutes," he said, as he took up a position about fifty yards in front of us. "I know one thing."

"What?" asked Jet.

"I should have brought an umbrella. I'm going to get my hair wet when I take my helmet off."

"Never mind that," said Jet. "Remember what we told you. Loosen your helmet first. If you feel no ill effects, lift it slightly, take a shallow breath and, if that's OK, take a bigger one."

"And if it isn't?"

"Then fasten your helmet, increase your oxygen supply and breathe deeply."

"Right," said Lemmy, "here I go. Unfastening helmet." He raised his hands and began to unloosen the screws at the neck. "Helmet loose," he reported. There was a pause.

"Well, Lemmy," said Jet, "can you breathe?"

There was another pause while we waited for Lemmy's answer. Finally, after what seemed an age, it came.

"Sorry, Jet, I wasn't trying; I was holding my breath. But I'll do it this time. Lifting helmet – now."

We heard him take a short breath and expel it rapidly.

"Now," said Jet, "lower your helmet, quick."

"Too late," came the retort, "it's lowered."

"Then how do you feel?"

"All right, up to now anyway."

"You're sure?"

"It's air," broke in Mitch, "it must be air."

"The effects might be delayed," I cautioned him.

"I'll have another go now," said Lemmy. "Take a deeper breath this time." We saw him lift his helmet from the front, heard him breathe in. "Ha," he said, relief in his voice, "it feels all right."

"Thank God for that," said Jet. "No peculiar sensations, Lemmy?"

"No."

"Are you sure?"

"Sure I'm sure. In fact I think I'll take my helmet right off."

"No, don't," warned Jet, but it was too late. Lemmy had already removed it and was holding it in his hand. We heard him breathing in and out deeply, then he began to laugh hysterically.

"I can breathe," he said, "without a helmet. I can breathe – the first good, clean breath of fresh air for nearly a month." He began to laugh louder. "Air," he said, "air – beautiful air."

"Strewth," said Mitch, "what's come over him? He's dancing."

And sure enough he was.

"The oxygen content must be too high," I suggested. "It's making him feel lively."

"Lemmy," called Jet, "put your helmet on. Do you hear?" But Lemmy ignored Jet's pleas and went on laughing and dancing. Then he began to take his suit off.

Jet was now getting desperate. "It must be air," he said; "but what on earth is Lemmy doing?" Lemmy, his ear-piece still attached to his head, replied for himself.

"I'm going to take a shower," he said, "that's what."

"A shower?" I doubted my ears.

"Yes, in the rain. Don't you realise it's nearly a month since we had a proper bath?"

"But isn't it cold out there, Lemmy?" I asked him.

"I wouldn't know. To me it feels like a warm spring day on Earth, and now I'm here I'm going to make the best of it. Why don't you come in? The water's lovely."

We looked at each other in amazement.

"Yes, Jet," I said finally, "why don't we? Either it's all right or it isn't and I wouldn't mind standing in that rain myself. In fact, the idea appeals to me very much."

"Yeah," said Mitch, just as enthusiastically. "Let's get out there, all of us. We're probably going to be here the rest of our lives anyway – we might as well get used to it. Come on."

"All right," said Jet. "Open up the hatch, Doc, and let's go."

"Do we take the suits?" I asked him.

"Suits? What do we need suits for? There's life on this planet, life very much as we know it, so let's go out and say hullo to it, just as we are."

It is now nearly a week since we landed on this planet and Lemmy left the ship and found the atmosphere breathable. Since then we have discovered many other things; that the water is drinkable, the temperature mild, and the rain unceasing. In many respects this planet is very much like Earth and the days are very nearly the same length, almost to the second. The cultivated area along the river banks contains a variety of crops, principally a kind of wheat or barley. But, whatever it is, it is in the early stages of its growth, which leads us to believe that we have arrived here during the late spring or early summer. Who or what it is that has cultivated the soil we have no idea, for, with the exception of flights of birds across the dark, cloudy sky, we have seen no living thing since we arrived here. At night the forest resounds with weird cries of some creature or other; the voices come echoing across the clearing and, carried by the wind, sound as though they are just outside the ship. Perhaps there is food to be had in the forest but, until we can be sure what kind of creatures live there, we dare not risk entering it.

With our rations almost used up, we had to find food from somewhere. We found it in the river. On the fifth day after landing, Jet and Mitch, armed with home-made nets and hooks, tried their luck at fishing. Much to the surprise and relief of us all, they were successful. They caught a fish that was not unlike salmon trout. It made a good meal, particularly as we had not consumed any hot food since leaving home. We have no galley on our ship so we had no opportunity of cooking anything fancy. We built a fire on the ground underneath the ship's belly to shelter it from the rain, and boiled our fish, after cutting it up into small pieces, in one of the metal ration boxes. We ate it, without the luxury of bread, potatoes or any kind of vegetable, with our fingers.

We spent the nights within the ship and, for our own safety, always closed the hatch before sleeping. We would have closed the main door, too, except that it used up so much power, and we were conserving all we could to keep at least one light burning at night.

"What do we do when the juice gives out?" said Mitch one day. "Go out and buy some candles?"

There were many problems we'd have to solve before long, a great many.

While three of us slept, one always kept watch. He went into the pilot's cabin where, seated in its chair, he had a fairly good view of the surrounding countryside through the transparent canopy. Most nights, with the clouds so low and the rain so heavy, there was very little for him to see.

Right now it was Jet's turn to take watch while the remainder of us turned in.

"Who follows me?" Jet asked.

"I do," I told him.

"All right, Doc," he said, "I'll wake you in a couple of hours."

Mitch and Lemmy climbed onto their bunks. I sat on mine until I had finished filling in my journal, then I, too, settled down to sleep.

I was awakened by Jet calling Mitch. "Hey, wake up," he was saying; but Mitch, who was always a heavy sleeper, wasn't to be roused so easily.

"What is it, Jet?" I asked, sitting up in my bunk.

"The rain – it's stopped."

"You didn't wake us up just to tell us that, did you?" grumbled Lemmy.

"No, I didn't," said Jet. "But the sky has cleared and I can see the stars."

"Well, what else did you expect?" asked Mitch, sleepily.

"But the constellations . . ."

"What about them, Jet?" I asked.

"They're the same as we would see from Earth."

"What?" Mitch sat up in his bunk, wide awake now. "They can't be."

"They are, I tell you. Come and look for yourselves."

"You bet we will," said Mitch.

We followed Jet to the pilot's cabin. But for a few scudding clouds, the sky was completely clear and out of its deep blue shone the familiar groups of stars we would normally recognise from the northern hemisphere of the Earth.

"They are the same," I said.

"Not quite the same," said Jet.

"How do you mean?" I asked him.

"Look at Lyra," he said.

I did, but the constellation looked exactly the same as the last time I had seen it. Vega, the arc lamp of the sky, shone in all its brilliance. Sulafat, Sheleak and Epsilon, the famous double double, all stood out clearly.

"I've been watching it for an hour or more," said Jet, "and in all that time Vega hasn't moved from that position, well, hardly; but the other stars have moved quite a distance. They're circling round her."

"You mean," I asked incredulously, "that Vega is the Pole Star?"

"That's just what I mean."

As everybody knows, the Pole Star is the one 'fixed' star in the heavens and marks the point where the north pole of the Earth points towards the sky. But Vega is not the Pole Star, at least, it wasn't the last time I saw it.

"I don't understand it," I told Jet.

"Well, I do," he replied, "at least, I think I do. Vega has been the Pole Star before and it will be again. Every 26,000 years or so it occupies the place we normally see occupied by Polaris."

"But," said Mitch, "apart from the displacement of Vega, the shapes of the constellations are exactly as we know them."

"Yes," conceded Jet, "but don't you see, only from the Earth, or maybe from some other part of the solar system, would the constellations assume the shapes they do."

"You mean we must be somewhere within the solar system?" queried Mitch.

"Yes."

"Well, that's a comfort," broke in Lemmy.

"And that's not all," said Jet slowly. "We know that within the solar system there is only one planet with air, trees, water, rain and clouds – the Earth. In other words, this can only be the Earth – it *is* the Earth."

"What?" I exclaimed.

"And I went through all that performance *testing* the air," said Lemmy in disgust.

"But if we are on the Earth," reasoned Mitch, "how do you account for the constellations being out of position? Why is Vega the Pole Star?"

"There is only one possible explanation," Jet considered his words carefully. "We've landed on the Earth all right, but at a different time from when we left it."

What Jet told us was so fantastic, so incomprehensible, that for a full minute none of us spoke. I was the first to break the silence.

"How different?"

"Heaven knows," said Jet, "but my guess is at least 13,000 years."

"Which way?" said Lemmy. "Forward or back?"

"I don't know – I just don't know."

Lemmy looked at Jet blankly. "You see," Jet went on, "the stars are constantly shifting and the pole of the heavens is continually moving, tracing a circle in the sky. We hardly notice any difference in a lifetime because the movement is so slow, but over a thousand years the change is quite considerable. Five thousand years ago, back from 1965, that is, the Pole Star was Thuban in Draco, as it was when the Egyptians built their Pyramids. Five thousand years on the Pole Star will be a star in the constellation Cepheus."

"And how many thousands of years from 1965 before it would be Vega?"

"I've already told you."

"You mean we've landed back on Earth either 13,000 years before or after we left it?"

"Not necessarily," said Jet. "It takes 26,000 years for the star that marks the Pole to make its complete circuit – 26,000 years between the time it is the Pole Star and the time it returns to that position."

"I don't see what you're driving at."

"Just this. How do we know how many *times* Vega has been the Pole Star since we left Earth?"

Lemmy paused while the full sense of what Jet had said sank in. Then he said, rather weakly, "You mean we might have to add another 26,000 years to the 13,000 we've already got?"

"Yes, Lemmy. Perhaps even more – it depends on how often the cycle has been completed."

"Don't, Jet. It sends me dizzy just thinking about it."

"All this is assuming we are on the Earth," said Mitch.

"Where else could we be?" asked Jet.

"I don't know, but if this is the Earth it should have a moon, a very large one, revolving round it."

"Yes, of course," I said.

"Then where is it?" demanded Mitch.

"Probably hasn't risen yet," said Jet, "or else it's already set. But since we've been here the Moon must have southed six times. We just haven't seen it, that's all."

"If we did," said Mitch, "it would make all the difference. It would be the final proof that we *are* back on Earth."

"We'll keep a watch for it," said Jet. "It may rise before dawn. If it doesn't, then we are bound to see it one evening soon, just after sunset."

We all decided to stay up with Jet. None of us could have slept anyway, we were too excited. An hour before sunrise our patience and vigilance were rewarded. The slim crescent of the old Moon rose above the horizon. We turned the telescope on it. Mitch took first look, then each of us in turn. Only a small area was illuminated by the Sun but, so far as we could tell, that was identical with the Moon with which we were familiar, which we had so recently left and last saw directly behind us, filling our televiewer screen. Grimaldi and other features of the eastern limb were clearly recognisable.

"Here," said Lemmy, as he removed his eye from the telescope, "I suppose there's no way the Moon could help us find out exactly what period of time we're in?"

"No, Lemmy," I told him. "I doubt if the features of the Moon have appreciably changed in 10,000 years."

"But there must be something we can do to find out. Or do we just sit here, worse off, for all our scientific knowledge, than those animals or whatever they are out there in the forest? At least they don't know that they don't know what age they're in."

"We have one clue," I suggested.

"What's that?" asked Mitch.

"The ice cap: it's large. We must have arrived here either at the beginning or the end of a glacial epoch."

"Oh, you mean the Ice Age," ventured Lemmy.

"Not *the* Ice Age, Lemmy," said Jet, "there were more than one of them. There are supposed to have been four. The first is estimated to have reached its peak 500,000 years ago."

"Seems like only yesterday."

"The second was 400,000 years ago, the third 150,000."

"And the fourth?"

"Assumed to have reached its maximum 50,000 years ago."

"So we could be somewhere in that period," I suggested.

"Could be," agreed Jet.

"Look," said Lemmy, "why bother about the thousands? A hundred years either way is enough to cut us off from life as we know it."

"Well, my guess is that we are somewhere between the fourth and fifth Ice Ages," said Jet, "always assuming there was to have been a fifth. I'd say 39,000 years or so before or after our own time."

"Only it isn't our time any more," I said.

"Well, I know one thing," put in Lemmy, "it must be back. If we had gone forward in time, the world wouldn't look like this."

"Why not?"

"Because over thousands of years man would have progressed. This would be a scientific world with great cities, controlled weather, roads, aeroplanes, space ships – but there's not a sign of anything, not even any living creature – except for the row we hear coming from the forest at night. We must be in the past."

"I wish I could be as sure of Man's future on Earth as you are, Lemmy," I told him, "but the way he was carrying on when we left, he could easily have destroyed himself by now, or the climatic conditions could have changed so much that his species died out altogether and another has taken its place."

"You mean we might be the only creatures of our kind on Earth, just the four of us?"

We have now been on this planet, which can only be the Earth, for 2 weeks. By now, we have got used to the idea. Our life is a peculiar mixture of the primitive and the scientific. Mitch spends most of his time within the ship, observing the heavens

*with the aid of the telescope, and the navigational tables. He
hopes, before long, to deduce our position. Finding our latitude
was easy: it is approximately 35°, so we might be anywhere
along a line drawn from North Africa eastwards through Asia
Minor, North India, China or North America. Meanwhile Jet,
Lemmy and I attend to the more immediate necessities of life.
We catch fish; in fact, we live on fish. So far we have found no
fruit or vegetable that we recognise or would risk eating.
Perhaps, later, there will be plenty of fruit to be had; certainly
the crops along the river bank must ripen within a few weeks. At
night we still take turns at keeping watch, listening to the
breathing of our companions and the cries of the nocturnal
creatures that inhabit the forest.*

One evening we were seated in the ship's cabin after supper,
discussing methods of preserving food should winter come.
Mitch had been rather silent throughout the meal.

"Something on your mind, Mitch?" Jet asked him.

"Yes," the engineer replied. "I think I've arrived at
something."

"About our position, you mean?"

"Yes."

"Good for you," said Jet. "Where are we?"

"Well, I just can't believe we can be where my calculations
say we are."

"And where's that?"

"In the Mediterranean, right smack in the middle of it."

"Do you mean the sea?" asked Lemmy, his eyes opening
wide at the thought.

"That's how it looks."

"Two weeks ago, with all that rain, I might have believed
you. But that country out there looks solid enough to me."

"You quite positive, Mitch?" I asked him.

"Well, I'll go through it all again if you like."

"No, wait," said Jet. "You could be right. It doesn't follow
that what was water, or will be water, in 1965 is water now."

"Of course it doesn't," I said.

"Was the Mediterranean ever known to be dry land?"

"Yes, Lemmy," said Jet. "Well, parts of it anyway."

"How long ago?"

"Fifty thousand years, maybe less. Thirty or even twenty five thousand."

"And that would line up with the ice theory, too," I said. "The fourth Ice Age was receding then."

"And what kind of animals were there?" It was Lemmy again.

"Oh, all kinds. Most of the animals that we knew in our age were in existence then. Others, like the mammoth and the sabre-toothed tiger, were rapidly dying out."

"Were there any men?" persisted Lemmy. "Like us, I mean?"

"Well," I told him, "it has been estimated that men, not very different from us, have inhabited some parts of the Earth for something like 200,000 years."

"Could they have planted those crops?"

"I doubt it," said Jet thoughtfully.

"Then who did plant them, and where are they, and when they turn up, what will they do to us?"

"That's something we'll only find out when it happens."

Another day has passed under a clear blue sky and in warm sunshine. But for our circumstances, life here could be very pleasant. There has still been no sign of the creatures, human or otherwise, that cultivate the fields along the banks of the river and, strangely enough, the crops don't seem to need any attention. They grow stronger and larger every day, and there are no weeds that we can see to choke them. In fact, they seem to thrive in ideal conditions which often makes me think that if we have moved in time at all, it is forward, to a period when knowledge of cultivation is so advanced that crops can be planted and then left to take care of themselves until harvest time.

It was on the morning of the tenth day that we caught our second glimpse of the ships that we had first seen nestled in the crater on the far side of the Moon. Jet and Lemmy had been collecting fuel for the fire and I had been cutting and cleaning the fish ready for the next meal. Only Mitch was inside the cabin, working on a plan for building a windmill to supply us with electricity.

I don't know what compelled me to look up when I did but there, high in the sky, picked out by the Sun, were about twenty brilliant spots of light in circular formation. They had appeared over the horizon beyond the forest and were rapidly climbing, tracing a large arc in the sky. Within a few moments, they were directly over our heads and there they stopped, poised above us. Excitedly I drew Jet's and Lemmy's attention to them.

"The telescope," said Jet urgently. "Let's get inside the ship and take a look at them." He ran towards the extended ladder as he spoke, with Lemmy and me hard on his heels.

Mitch got a bit of a fright as we went crashing into the cabin. He thought at first that some animal was chasing us. But when we explained what we had seen, he immediately dashed into the pilot's cabin to take a look for himself. Meanwhile Jet was already in the astrodome.

"They're still directly above us," he said, as he adjusted the telescope, "and there's the same blue light flashing on and off underneath every one of them."

"They must be observing us," I suggested. "Why else should they hang up there like that?"

"Well, let them take a good look," said Lemmy, "then maybe they'll do something about us."

"What?" I asked.

"How should I know? But they've never been short of ideas before, have they? I know," he said suddenly, "perhaps they've come to help us. Maybe they realise they've put us down in quite the wrong place and now want to take us back again."

"Don't be ridiculous," I told him. "How could they do that?"

"By the same methods as they got us here, of course. We take off and reach free orbit and they surround us, see. Then they do whatever it is they did before, but this time they reverse the process and – whoops – we're back where we started, on our way home from the Moon, back in 1965."

"This ship isn't big enough to take off and reach free orbit," I told Lemmy. "Not from the Earth, she's not. She needs a booster stage full of fuel, and we haven't got one and no hope of ever getting one."

"But with the power those ships have, perhaps we don't even need to go that high. Maybe all we need to do is take off and they'll do the rest."

I didn't answer him.

"You don't want to, do you?" Lemmy raised his voice, appealing to Jet and Mitch. "None of you do. But you can't want to stay here for the rest of your lives, with mammoths and things trampling all over your backyard."

Of course we didn't, but there was nothing we could do to prevent it, so far as we could see.

The strange craft were still hovering above us, motionless. Mitch, from the pilot's canopy, and Jet, from his position at the telescope, continued to watch them.

"I'm sorry, Lemmy," I said after a long silence, "the only thing we can depend on this ship for now is to get from one part of the globe to another. She'll never travel through space again."

A faint gleam of hope brightened Lemmy's face. "Then why can't we do just that – go to England at least, London maybe."

"Because there isn't any London, Lemmy. Almost certainly the whole of Britain, as far down as the Thames, is ice-covered, frozen solid."

A sudden cry from Jet told us that the ships were now on the move again. Lemmy and I rushed over to the pilot's canopy to see them for ourselves. Sure enough the circle of bright silver dots was now moving rapidly westwards. A few minutes later it had disappeared below the horizon and we saw our fleeting visitors no more. We all returned to the centre of the cabin but none of us could find anything to say.

"Well," said Lemmy at last, "maybe I'd better start cooking the fish. It is my turn, isn't it?"

"Cheer up, Lemmy," said Jet. "This may not be as bad as it looks."

"I hope it's not as bad as you look, nor as bad as any of us look. I'll just resign myself to the fact that I've got to learn to be a caveman and like it."

That night it was Lemmy's turn to take first watch in the pilot's cabin. He was his own, cheerful self again and, while I was preparing for bed, came over to my bunk for a chat.

"You know," he said, "all things considered, I don't think this need be such a bad life."

"You think not, Lemmy?" I asked.

"Well, it could be one long holiday. We're not responsible to anybody but ourselves. We can do what we like when we like and nobody to tell us no."

"That's the danger," I told him. "It would pall after a bit, I'm sure."

"Oh, I don't know," said Lemmy. "A few months from now and we might be quite proud of ourselves. We might even start an entirely new kind of civilisation."

"We might," I told him, "but there'd be nobody to carry it on."

"No, there wouldn't, would there?" said Lemmy disconsolately.

Then he put his hand into the breast pocket of his crew suit. "Doc," he said as he did so.

"Yes, Lemmy?" I asked him.

"About what you said just now."

"Well?"

"If I hung this over my bunk, would it matter?" He pulled a photograph out and showed it to me. It was a picture of Becky, his girl.

"Why should it?" I asked him.

"Well, I usually keep it in my pocket, but I thought it might make the place look more homely if I hung it up."

"I'm sure it would, Lemmy."

"I wonder what she's doing now," he said, gazing at the photograph. "You know, Doc, I never did tell her where I was going, but she found out once we'd landed on the Moon – what with my picture in all the papers. I told her the day I got back to London I was going to take her out and give her the time of her life. We were going to paint the town red and I was going to give her a bit of rock I'd picked up from the Moon's surface as a souvenir. And now look at the mess we're in. There's her picture and, so far as I know, she's not even born yet."

"No," I said.

"Then how can I have her picture?" said Lemmy brightly. "Doc, do you think she is alive, I mean at the same time as we are – you know, everything going on at once like the pages in a book?"

"I don't quite see what you're getting at, Lemmy."

"Well, supposing you've got a book and you're just sitting down to read it."

"Well?"

"You begin at chapter one and start ploughing your way through, don't you?"

"Yes."

"Well, you can't read chapter seven until you've read the first six chapters, but that doesn't mean chapter seven doesn't exist. You just haven't reached it yet."

"Sure," I said.

"Well, couldn't time be like that? I mean, the normal thing is to start at the beginning and go on, but I suppose it is possible to skip a few pages, or even turn back a few. Maybe that's what's happened to us. Somebody or something's taken us out of the page where we belong and planted us here on an earlier one, but the other pages are still there. Henry the Eighth is marrying his sixth wife on his proper page and, in our proper place, we are taking off for the Moon or just going to – it all depends on what page you're at and what part of it you happen to have reached."

"You mean there's no such thing as time really. Everything happens at once."

"Yes, in a way."

"Then we must be careful if ever we get back to our right page, as you call it, that we don't run into ourselves."

"Eh?"

"I think I'd better get some sleep, Lemmy. We've got enough problems without worrying about the true nature of time."

"Yes, Doc," he said, and went over to the pilot's canopy to take over his watch.

Chapter 11
THE VOICE

We were roused by Lemmy shouting at the top of his voice as he came rushing out of the pilot's cabin and into the main quarters.

"For heaven's sake," called Jet, "what are you yelling about?"

"There's something outside," said Lemmy, "coming out of the forest."

"What?" asked Mitch sceptically.

"I don't know, a sort of tank. It's coming towards us, I tell you, and a bright light keeps flashing on and off."

Jet pushed Lemmy to one side and made for the pilot's cabin. A second or two later, Mitch and I had joined him, but all we saw was the distant forest outlined against the starry sky.

"Are you sure you saw something, Lemmy?" demanded Jet.

"Of course I'm sure. That thing was there, I tell you, and when the light came on it lit up the countryside for miles around, like a sheet of lightning."

"Maybe that's just what it was," said Mitch. "Perhaps there's a storm blowing up."

"There's not a cloud in the sky," Jet pointed out.

"Tell us exactly what you thought you saw, Lemmy," I told him.

"Well, I was sitting in the cabin and . . ."

He got no farther. At that precise moment a brilliant flash of light penetrated the pilot's canopy and shone full into our faces. Mitch and I instinctively leapt back into the cabin, falling over in our haste. Jet, who was seated in the pilot's chair, wasn't as quick as us and when he did make it he tripped over Mitch who was lying on the floor.

"Get down, quick," said Jet, "all of you."

I made my way to the table and groped along the panelling until I found the pilot's door control. I pressed it, there was a whirr, and the door closed.

"The main door, Doc," Jet called. "Can you find the switch?" A few more moments' groping, and the main door closed, too.

None of us could see. The powerful light had blinded us. This was the last straw. To be stranded, as we were, and to be blind as well was more than I could take. I felt like beating on the control table with my fists. And then, much to my surprise and relief, I began to see things again, dimly illuminated by the single bulb which supplied our cabin with light. Slowly my sight returned.

"I don't think there's anything to worry about," I said, trying to reassure the others; "it was a bright light and our eyes had got used to the darkness. It was bound to blind us temporarily."

"It was like looking directly into the Sun," said Lemmy. "All I can see are bright green patches."

"I'm beginning to see better now," said Jet, "and there's certainly no pain."

"What kind of light was it?" I asked.

"Maybe some kind of super searchlight," volunteered Mitch.

"That's what you think," said Lemmy.

"What's your idea then?"

"A death ray."

"What?"

"You've heard of them, haven't you?"

"Of course we've heard of them," said Mitch, "been hearing about them for years, but no one has ever got round to perfecting one yet."

"Not in our time," said Lemmy, "back in 1965. But we're not back in 1965. There could be a death ray now."

"Then why aren't we dead?" Jet remarked flatly.

"Oh," said Lemmy, "that's a point, isn't it?"

"Whatever it was," Jet went on, "it doesn't seem to have done us any harm."

"That doesn't mean it won't," said Lemmy pessimistically.

"What's that thing doing out there?"

"Well, none of us is going out to look, that's certain," said Jet. "We'll remain in here until it's gone."

"And when do you think that will be?" asked Mitch. "How do we know it's still out there anyway?"

"We don't. We'll wait a couple of hours. If nothing has happened in that time, we'll open up the pilot's cabin and risk another look."

"How about the televiewer?" I suggested.

We had not used the televiewer since we landed but on the last inspection it had been in working order. But it was not working now and it was half an hour before Lemmy managed to bring the screen to life. When, at last, the camera was rotated, there was nothing unusual to be seen outside.

"They must have gone away," said Jet. He sounded almost disappointed.

After an hour of rotating the camera at ten-minute intervals, Jet decided to open up the pilot's cabin door and take a look through the window. This we did, but, even with the wider range of vision this gave us, we could still see no sign of anything unusual.

"Well," I said at last, "there's only one way to be sure now and that is to go out there and look."

"Very well, Doc," Jet said. "Get a flashlight and we'll go."

When we reached the main door, Jet turned on the flashlight and slowly threw the beam round a considerable area. Then he almost dropped the torch in surprise for it illuminated three deep furrows which completely encircled the ship. They were about three feet in diameter, just as deep, and the distance between each furrow was about six feet. They appeared to have been made by heavy spheres. We could only conclude they were made by the 'wheels' of the tank that Lemmy had seen.

"It seems to have gone round us once and then made off again," I said to Jet.

"Yes," he said as he flashed the light over a wider area. Then I heard him draw his breath. "Doc," he said abruptly, "I'm going out there."

"No, Jet," I remonstrated, "Not now, wait until daylight."

But he ignored my protest and ordered Lemmy to let down the ladder. I watched with apprehension as he made his way over to the remains of the fire on which we had cooked our last meal. Then he stooped, picked something up from the ground and returned to the ship.

"All right, Doc," he said, as he climbed into the airlock. "Now let's get back."

Once in the cabin, Jet went straight to the control table and threw on it the object he had found outside. We all gathered round and gazed at it curiously.

"What's that?" asked Mitch.

"Take a look at it," said Jet. "You tell me."

Mitch picked it up and turned it over in his hands. "Just a fancy piece of stone," he said, without much interest.

"Doesn't its shape tell you anything?"

"It's a peculiar shape all right, but . . ."

"Take hold of it," Jet broke in, "feel the weight and balance of it in your hand. I'd say it was some kind of a weapon."

"Let me see it," I asked Mitch, and took the stone from him.

"Somebody made that thing and dropped it near the ship some time after we came in," Jet went on.

"How do you know?" asked Lemmy.

"Because of where I found it. It was right in the very place where I was sitting earlier, near the fire. If it had been there then, I'd have noticed it, wouldn't I?"

"You could hardly have helped yourself, could you?" Lemmy said.

I examined the object. It was almost a foot long and shaped rather like an aspidistra leaf. The handle was flat and narrow. The leaf-shaped blade was about half an inch thick and tapered off at the edges and to a point at its tip. One edge was certainly sharp, the other blunt. It had been roughly chipped into shape and then, apparently, rubbed down until it was almost smooth. When held in the hand, it had a nice balance and could be used either as a dagger or some kind of chopper. I handed it back to Jet.

"It's some kind of knife all right," I told him, "and, for what it is, very craftily made. It's been used recently, too."

"How do you know?" said Lemmy.

"Look," I pointed at the knife, "you see those dark patches there? Blood."

"Eh? Whose?"

"How should I know? Maybe whoever dropped it used it for hunting or something."

"Let me have another look, Jet," said Mitch.

"Sure," said Jet, and he handed the object to the engineer.

Mitch admitted, a little grudgingly I thought, that it might have been a knife. "But I've never seen one like this before," he added.

"Except in history books," said Jet.

"How do you mean?"

"For thousands of years Man was making just this kind of weapon, certainly in Europe and the Mediterranean regions. Even the ancient Egyptians used them until they discovered the use of metal."

"You mean this is a relic from the Stone Age?" Mitch queried. "But it's in such darned good condition, and Doc says it's been used only recently."

"Precisely."

"But that would suggest that out there, outside this ship," Mitch carried on, "there are men or some kind of animals who use stone knives, who belong to a stone age."

"Why not? We might have landed anywhere – anywhere in time."

"But it doesn't make sense," argued Mitch. "That presupposes two entirely different civilisations existing at once. One extremely advanced, with machines and space ships, the other as primitive as prehistory itself."

"Could be," I suggested. "Railroads were spanning the American continent at the same time as Red Indians were still living in a primitive state, still in a stone age."

"I don't know what to make of it," said Jet. "I only know this knife was outside."

"Did whoever dropped it leave any footprints behind?" I asked him.

"Not that I noticed, but the grass round that fire has been trampled flat by us anyway."

"Well," I said, "maybe we'll get to the bottom of it some day."

"Meanwhile," said Jet, "we'd better get back to sleep. We have a busy day ahead of us."

We had planned to do a little exploring and next morning; in spite of the events of the previous night, we decided to go ahead with the project. We intended to cover an area about a mile in radius with the ship as its centre. Only Jet and Mitch were to go and they were to keep in constant touch with Lemmy and me with the aid of their personal radios.

"I only hope the batteries can stand up to it," said Lemmy. "There can't be much juice left in them now. And what if you meet up with any of those ape men with the stone knives?"

"I'm almost hoping we will," said Mitch. "It might clear up a few things."

"And what if that machine comes back?" said Lemmy. He was in a pessimistic mood this morning.

"We can't stay locked up in here for ever," said Mitch. "We've got to know what lies beyond the horizon."

Two minutes later Mitch and Jet were outside the ship, checking the radios. They still seemed quite healthy.

"Hearing you loud and clear," came Jet's voice.

"Me, too," said Mitch.

"Then I think we'll get started," said Jet, "and I . . ." He broke off.

"I don't think you'd better," said Lemmy urgently. "You'd better come back into the ship, and quick."

"Too right we will," said Mitch.

There was good reason for the new panic – the space music was back again.

I ran over to the main door control and closed it behind Jet and Mitch as they entered the airlock. By the time they had reached the cabin, the noise was at its greatest.

"Well," shouted Lemmy above the racket, "that's put paid to a nice morning's stroll."

"It must be those ships again," I exclaimed, "and they must be very close."

Mitch was all for looking out of the pilot's window but Jet refused to allow it in case the 'ray', or whatever it was, might be projected at us again. He ordered me to close the door and, by the time I had, the music had stopped.

"The televiewer, Lemmy," said Jet; "see if it's working."

"Shouldn't think so," said Lemmy helpfully, but switched on just the same. Within a few moments the screen was glowing and a picture of the country towards the river was clearly visible.

"Rotate the camera," ordered Jet. Lemmy did, and there outside, not a hundred yards away, was another space ship identical with the one which had landed in the crater on the Moon.

It was the same episode all over. Once more the strange music was heard and the opening in the dome of the craft revealed itself, only this time the ladder which Mitch had found on the opposite side of the craft was facing us.

"Looks like they're inviting us to go out there and get in," said Mitch.

"Well, if they are," said Jet positively, "we're not accepting."

"Maybe," I suggested, "this time somebody will come out."

"Don't, Doc," said Lemmy.

"Well, why not?" I asked him.

"Then whoever it is must have two legs."

"I don't see why."

"Who else could use a ladder?"

"A cat can climb a ladder," I reminded him.

Lemmy didn't reply. And nothing came out. Thirty minutes later a constant watch had revealed no further development in the situation.

"Well," said Mitch, "what are we going to do – sit here all day biting our finger nails? Supposing that thing stays out there for a week, what do we do about food?"

"I know," said Jet suddenly, "the radio."

"The radio?" repeated Mitch, looking very puzzled.

"Yes, don't you remember? When you went up to that ship before and kicked it, we all heard it over the radio. And when you went inside, we heard your voice. Obviously if that ship can communicate with us at all," concluded Jet, "it must be via the radio. Lemmy, is the transmitter still switched on?"

"Yes, Jet."

"But the last time," protested Mitch, "I had to be in there before you heard anything."

"Who knows what will happen this time? At least it's worth a try."

Mitch agreed, reluctantly. "Yes, I suppose it is." He had hardly finished speaking when over the intercom speaker we heard the space music once again, but this time it didn't increase in volume.

Quite suddenly it stopped.

"Well," said Lemmy, "is that all we get? That's nothing new."

And then to our surprise and consternation, we heard something that was. It wasn't very loud but it was sufficient to give us a violent shock. It was a voice.

"Hullo, Luna," it said.

"Blimey!" said Lemmy. "Did you hear that?"

"Quiet," said Jet.

"But it was a voice."

"A human voice," I added.

"And it came over the radio," said Mitch.

"Yes," said Jet. "It came from there." He pointed at the image on the televiewer screen. "There's somebody or something in that ship."

The voice was completely characterless. "Hullo, Luna," was delivered very precisely, rather as one used to hear on the elevators in the old London subways when a disembodied voice announced: 'Stand clear of the doors'. It was neither friendly, antagonistic, calm nor excited; it was just a voice.

None of us said a word or moved a muscle for at least two minutes. It was Jet who broke the silence eventually and all he did was to repeat slowly what he had said a moment before:

"It came from there. There's somebody or something in that ship."

"And whoever it is," said Lemmy, who had recovered his tongue by now, "he speaks English."

"Wouldn't it be rather awkward if I didn't?" There was no tone of interrogation in the announcement. It was only the order in which the words were put that made it a question.

"Who are you?" asked Jet. "What do you want?"

"We only want to help you," came the dispassionate reply.

"How?"

"All we ask is for you to leave your ship and enter ours. No harm will come to you – you need not be afraid."

"We're not afraid," said Jet, "just cautious."

"Speak for yourself," said Lemmy quietly.

"Are you anything to do with that ship we saw on the Moon?" asked Jet.

"Yes, we are."

"Then who are you?" asked Mitch.

The Voice ignored the question. "Leave your own ship and come in here."

"You come in here," suggested Lemmy. "Why don't you show yourself?"

"I cannot show myself."

"Why not?" asked Lemmy. "Are you invisible?"

"No, but I am not in this ship."

Jet turned to Mitch and me. "What are we going to do about this?" he said.

Lemmy left us in no doubt as to what he wanted to do about it. "Stay where we are, of course," he said. "It would be barmy to go out there."

"Not necessarily," I told him. "No harm came to Mitch when he went into the ship we saw on the Moon."

"Well," said Mitch doubtfully, "at least I wasn't conscious of anything strange going on."

"But if all of us go into that ship," Lemmy argued, "who knows what might happen?"

"I think we should find out more about this before we even set foot outside," said Jet. "I'll talk to him. Hullo, whoever you are," he called. "We would like you to answer a few questions."

"Then go ahead."

"Well, in the first place, have you anything to do with our being here now?"

"Possibly."

"That's a great help," said Mitch.

"And how about that perishing music we keep hearing?" asked Lemmy. "Is that anything to do with you?"

"Music?"

"Yes, music."

"What is music?" said the Voice flatly.

"You don't know – what – music is?"

167

"No."

"Well, it's a kind of – noise," Lemmy groped for his words, "that goes up and down – and when you hear it, well, it makes you feel good. Except your music – that makes you feel dreadful."

"A noise, you say?"

"Yes," said Jet, "a peculiar kind of noise."

"Like this?" And over the radio came a short burst of the weird music we'd now heard so often. It started, as usual, with a high-pitched note, swooped down to a deep, almost inaudible bass and died away in reverberating echoes.

At the end of the short interlude Jet said excitedly, "Yes, that's it, that's it exactly. And whenever we hear it, something always happens to us."

"What is it?" asked Mitch. "What does it do?"

"All I did was turn on the power."

"The power that drives your ship?" asked Mitch.

"Then it was you on the Moon, wasn't it?" Jet gave the Voice no chance to answer Mitch's question.

"One of our ships visited your side of the Moon."

"Weren't you in it?"

"No."

"You mean those ships were remote controlled, and you sent them specially to look for us?"

"No, we didn't. We were very surprised to find you there."

"Not half so surprised as we were to find you," broke in Lemmy.

"Then where are you from?" asked Jet.

"From the other side of the universe."

"That's just what Mitch told us, remember?" I said.

"Leave your own ship and come into ours."

"Look," said Jet politely, "will you give us a few minutes to talk this thing over?"

"Certainly."

"Can we call you back?"

"There is really no need, I cannot go away."

"Then you don't mind if we switch off our radios. We have to conserve power."

"When you call, I will answer."

Jet turned to address all of us. "Switch off your sets," he commanded. We did so. "Well," he went on, "what do you make of it?"

"We must go out there," said Mitch eagerly. "Just think of what we could learn from those – whatever they are. Why, just to have the secret of their motive power alone would be worth the risk."

"In many ways I agree," I told him, "but if they can help us, as they say they can, why can't they do it here and now? Why do we have to go into their ship and, if we do, where will they take us?"

"That's what worries me," put in Lemmy quickly.

"Well, it's something we can ask him," said Jet.

"Go on then," prompted Lemmy, "see what he says."

"Right," said Jet. "Switch on the radio."

Lemmy did. "Hullo, hullo – can you hear me?"

"Yes," said the Voice.

"If we enter that thing," asked Jet, "what will happen to us?"

"The ship will take off."

"Where to?"

"Not very far."

"Then why can't you come to us?" asked Jet.

"It is safer this way. You are in great danger where you are."

"What kind of danger?"

"Look," broke in Mitch impatiently, "why bother with all this? If we're going, let's go."

"Quiet, Mitch," ordered Jet. "We'll go when we're good and ready."

"All right," said Mitch disagreeably, "have your natter, but hurry up."

Jet ignored him and again addressed the Voice. "Tell me one thing more."

"Yes?"

"This danger you speak of; is it a threat to us personally or to our ship?"

"I don't think your ship is likely to come to harm, but you probably will, and very soon."

"Come *on*, Jet" said Mitch. "He couldn't say much more, could he?"

The Voice was obviously listening to our conversation and, for the first time, interrupted it. "If you don't like where we shall take you, you can always return," it said.

"All right. Give us a few minutes to get ready and we'll come."

"And bring your radios with you. They are our only means of communication at the moment."

"Very well," said Jet. "I'll call you again when we're outside."

We entered the airlock and, by means of the remote control button, closed the cabin hatch. From outside there was no way of closing the main door or of stowing the ladder which led down from it, but we felt fairly confident that no normal person could penetrate our ship farther than the airlock because of its strong, hermetically-sealed door.

We climbed down to the ground and, rather slowly I must admit, made our way towards the circular-shaped ship where it stood silent and forbidding between us and the river.

Chapter 12
SPACE CRAFT

Three minutes later we were standing before the strange space craft and the first thing Lemmy did was to kick it. "Just want to make sure this thing is solid," he said, "and that the whole thing isn't just a dream."

"I'd better go first," said Jet. "Keep your radios on and I'll tell you if it's OK to follow."

Jet climbed the ladder. When he reached the top, he paused for a few moments and then entered the door of the dome.

"Hullo, can you hear me?"

"Yes, Jet," said Mitch.

"What's it like in there?" asked Lemmy.

"Seems to be exactly the same kind of ship Mitch went into. I don't think there's anything to worry about here."

For a moment my mind went back to that time on the Moon when, in an identical situation, Mitch had used almost the same words. On that occasion plenty had transpired to worry us.

"You'd better come up," said Jet. So, hoping for the best, I followed Mitch and Lemmy up the ladder. A few moments later the four of us were standing in the cabin of the strange ship.

We had hardly time to glance around us before we felt the ship trembling slightly. We looked at each other anxiously except for Mitch, to whom this was no new experience.

"This is it," he exclaimed. "This is the same vibration I felt when I said the ship came to life, just before the dome closed."

"That's just what it is doing," said Lemmy, pointing towards the shutter which was now rapidly blocking out the daylight.

For a moment we were in total darkness and then, like the crescent of a new moon, an arc of light appeared at our feet. Rapidly the arc widened and I realised a sliding hatch was opening in the floor. The light came from a compartment below ours. The arc became a circle, about three feet in diameter, and we saw a ladder leading below.

"Why do you stand there?" we heard the Voice say suddenly. "Why don't you go down? Until you do the ship won't take off."

"Why can't it take off with us up here?" asked Lemmy.

"It can if you wish, but you would find it most uncomfortable. Do you prefer to stay where you are?"

"I prefer to get out altogether."

"No, Lemmy," said Jet. "Come along," he indicated to the rest of us, "I'll lead the way." And with that he began to descend the ladder.

Mitch, who was behind me, had not got half way down before the hatch closed above his head, sealing us off completely. Even if we wished to go back, we no longer had any choice in the matter.

The lower cabin was part of a large sphere, the upper half being the dome from which we had just descended. It was lit by diffused lighting, as though the very walls were aglow. Apart from the ladder, the only other visible object was a pedestal which stood on a black, shining globe, which might have been made of glass. Set in one wall was another large, octagonal-shaped panel with the now familiar series of buttons situated above it.

Mitch walked over to the panel. "Some kind of control table," he said.

"But why have control panels in a ship that's remote controlled?" asked Jet.

"Maybe it isn't all the time," said Mitch. "Our own ship was remote-controlled during take-off from Earth, but we've handled it ourselves ever since."

"Well, don't get too inquisitive," said Jet.

By this time Mitch was looking at the black, shiny sphere on the pedestal. None of us had a clue what it was for. It occurred to me that with the exception of the ladder and the octagonal-shaped panels set in the wall, everything about this strange craft was on a circular pattern; the ship itself was round, shaped like a doughnut, the roof was a dome, the hatch circular and the cabin spherical. The ship was of a most unusual design.

There were no windows and yet the air seemed fresh and clean. We concluded that there must be some kind of air-conditioner but could find no trace of it.

"Well, at least that means whoever built this ship needs to breathe, same as we do," Lemmy remarked.

"I don't think they can be all that different from us," I suggested, "or they couldn't exist on Earth at all."

"We haven't seen anybody yet, Doc," said Mitch, "only heard a voice."

"That's a point," said Jet. "They may be very different from us – exist in quite a different way. Look at this place. No seats, no couches, no food, no water, nothing."

"Here," said Lemmy, "perhaps they don't exist physically at all."

"Then how come they need physical ships?" asked Mitch.

"Just because they build them, it doesn't mean to say they've got to fly in them, any more than a meteorologist flies in a weather balloon."

"But always supposing that they do have some kind of physical shape," I suggested, "they're probably much tougher than us. "Maybe that's why their ships can fly so fast, and manoeuvre so easily. If they start throwing this thing around, they'll probably kill us all."

"Yes, but do *they* realise that?" asked Lemmy anxiously. "Do they know exactly how much the human body can stand?"

The possibilities suggested by Lemmy's remark were all too clear.

"You'd better try and contact them, Jet."

"Tell them to take it easy," said Lemmy. "Tell them we're weak, very weak."

Jet switched on his radio. "Hullo, hullo, can you hear me? Hullo."

There was no reply.

"Try him again."

"Hullo, Luna calling. Can you hear me?" He paused. "The set's dead, I can't hear a thing."

"Maybe not," Lemmy said quickly, "but I can feel something."

"And so can I," said Mitch. "The ship's on the move – in a vertical climb."

"Hullo, hullo," shouted Jet.

"Oh," moaned Lemmy, "we'll be squashed flat."

"Hullo. Hullo."

"We'd better lie down," said Mitch urgently, "all of us."

The pressure was increasing rapidly now and Jet joined the rest of us on the floor. After a while the ship ceased to climb and the pressure ended. But we hadn't stopped moving. Our course had merely changed from a vertical to a horizontal one. We had panicked over nothing and all felt rather foolish.

"Well, do we lie here all day?" asked Lemmy.

Jet was trying to call the Voice again but without success. "Somebody else had better have a go," he said.

"I'll try," I told him. "Hullo, hullo – come in please," I said, with an unusual tone of politeness. But it made no difference. There was still no reply.

"My set's dead, too," said Mitch. "I don't think any of them are working."

"Then it can't be the batteries, can it?" said Lemmy. "They wouldn't all run down at the same time."

"I've got it," said Jet. "Whatever power drives this ship must neutralise all the electronic equipment we're carrying."

"You mean," asked Lemmy, "that whenever the radio cut it was because one of these ships was around?"

"It's as likely an explanation as any."

"Then that would account for the fact that nothing worked before take-off on the Moon. Ships like this must have been all round us," I said.

"What else could it have been? I bet the minute this ship stops, the radios will work again."

"I don't know about that, but something's working over here," said Mitch. "This darned goldfish bowl is beginning to glow. There's a picture taking shape."

'Picture' was hardly the right word, for there, inside the bowl, we could see the river, the forest and the cultivated fields of the country we had just left, in three dimensions, and full colour. Slowly the scene rolled by, trees, river, other objects disappearing through the glass wall on one side, while fresh objects moved into view, apparently, through the other. We watched the contraption in silence, fascinated.

"Good heavens, a three-dimensional televiewer. This is a reproduction of the country we're flying over. That's why it's moving. I don't know what kind of beings they are that built this ship," Jet went on, "but they're way ahead of our time – streets ahead."

Very soon the forest gave way to a large, open plain. And then below us appeared a host of dome-shaped buildings. Quite suddenly there was a sensation in my stomach that told me we were falling towards the ground and falling very rapidly. Our knees buckled and we all collapsed in a heap. A few seconds later the gentlest of bumps told us we had landed. Mitch was sick.

Lemmy, in spite of his pale face, still tried to joke. "This must be where we change," he said.

We must have lain on the floor for fully fifteen minutes before we felt well enough to take an interest in what was happening to us. Then the hatch in the ceiling opened and a shaft of daylight shining through it told us the dome had opened, too.

"This is obviously where we're expected to get out," I said.

"Wait a minute; don't be in such a hurry." It was the Voice.

"Oh, there you are," said Lemmy. "We've been trying to call you."

"I'm sorry. Your radios don't function while our ship is in operation."

"We discovered that for ourselves, thanks," said Lemmy perkily.

"If they did, we would have been able to contact you before," the Voice went on. "We tried constantly. Even while you were out in space. When you were on the Moon we sent a ship to communicate with you, but you didn't respond."

"Is that what all that tapping was?"

"We were trying to decide what your ship was made of and how it operated."

"You have plenty of things we wish to know about, too, said Jet, "your ships and the power that drives them, and, above all, your apparent ability to travel through time. That is still no more than a theory where we come from in the twentieth century."

"You cannot travel through time?"

"Well, no, not wittingly."

"Then how do you travel from one part of the universe to another?"

"We don't. The farthest we ever got was from the Earth to the Moon. And we got back again, but, due to you, with disastrous results. We don't belong here, this is not our world."

"It is not ours either."

"Then what are you doing here?" asked Jet.

"Thousands of Earth years ago we began to colonise this globe."

"Colonise it?" asked Mitch. "Why?"

"Our own planet is dead. We can never return to it."

"Why not?"

"Its sun blew up."

"Eh?" interjected Lemmy.

"Once," went on the Voice, "it was a star like your sun, with planets – life-supporting planets – revolving round it. And then it began to expand, became a giant red star of such colossal size that it extended far beyond the orbits of the planets and consumed them. Our home was roasted out of existence."

"Then how did you get away?" queried Jet.

"Long before our world was threatened we had learned how to travel through space, but only to planets within our own system. As the day of destruction drew nearer, we were compelled to find a means of escaping from our sun altogether. It was then that we learned to travel through time."

"Then why didn't you travel backwards?" I asked, "back to the time before your sun began to expand?"

"We did."

"Didn't that solve your problem?"

"How would you like to live yesterday all over again, do exactly the same things in exactly the same way and be denied the knowledge and experience that the future has to offer?"

"It could get very dull," I admitted.

"It's abominable. We soon learned the only way was forward, so forward we went, across the universe, looking for a new planet, a place to live, a pleasant place, with a young sun and all the elements necessary to life."

"And you found it?" asked Jet.

"Yes, here, the Earth. When we arrived life was already firmly established. This was the most beautiful, the most hospitable planet we had ever discovered."

"So you settled here?" suggested Jet.

"Yes."

"How do you like it?" asked Lemmy.

"At first, very much, but now the time has come for us to leave once again, to find another planet like Earth, but one that doesn't contain the threat of its own destruction as this does."

"You mean our sun's expanding?" asked Lemmy anxiously.

"No. The danger that exists on Earth now, that is about to drive us away, wasn't here when we first came."

"What is it?" Jet asked.

"It must be very powerful to drive you away," I added.

"It is very powerful," replied the Voice, "something we cannot fight against."

"Then what is it?" persisted Jet.

"You will know soon enough. But now it's time for you to come outside and meet us, or what is left of us."

"Eh," said Lemmy.

"And don't be too surprised by what you see. We are very unlike you. We are not of this Earth. Life on our own planet was different and we have developed differently. You can have no idea of how we look."

"Er – now wait a minute – " Lemmy turned to Jet. "Can't he give us some idea of what he looks like first?"

"It might be as well," I said.

"Call him," said Lemmy. "Ask him to show himself on the televiewer at least."

Jet called but could get no reply. For fully five minutes we tried to raise the Voice, but to no avail.

"He should be hearing us," said Jet, "there's no music on. Perhaps he doesn't intend to answer."

"Maybe," said Lemmy. "He's probably afraid the sight of him will horrify us so much we'll want to go back."

"Then why bring us here in the first place?" queried Mitch.

"That's what's bothering me," said Lemmy. "For all we know the minute we step outside we'll be pounced on and locked up in a cage."

"Why in a cage?" asked Jet.

"Because we're different from him, that's why. We interest him. I expect his local zoo will make a lot of money with us shut up in it, like a lot of apes. Can't you see them, gathering round and poking us with sticks?"

"We don't know if they realise what a zoo is, Lemmy, least of all money," I said.

"All right, as scientific specimens then. What would our scientists say if they found some kind of animal they had never seen before? They wouldn't give it a banana and send it home, would they? They'd have it all nicely locked up in no time. It wouldn't matter what the animal felt about it."

"Well," suggested Jet, "we could at least go as far as the door and see if we fancy going any further." And with that, he began to climb the ladder to the upper cabin.

What we saw when we reached the opening was no horrible monster. In fact we saw no living creature of any kind, except a flight of birds flapping its way across the sky. Stretched out before us as far as the eye could see was the great array of domes. If each were a complete sphere then exactly half of it was below the ground.

"The place certainly seems deserted," said Jet.

"They're probably keeping out of sight," said Lemmy, "waiting to grab us when it's too late for us to go back."

"If they intended to be violent, they could have come into the ship. Now let's get down to ground level."

"If only we had a gun or something," said Lemmy, as he descended the ladder.

"You don't need guns to explore a lifeless world," said Mitch.

"This is no lifeless world."

"No, but the Moon is and it was the Moon we set out to explore."

"Now," said Jet, "keep close together and we'll go over to that town or whatever it is. And keep your radios on all the time in case the Voice calls us."

Ten minutes later we were wandering through the strange city. There were no streets or pavements. The domes rose straight out of the ground, which was still in its natural state.

Suddenly our tour was brought to a stop by a frightening roar. The shock was so great, I stood rooted to the spot – petrified. It had come from behind us. We turned, and there, not thirty yards away, its head down and tail lashing, was a horrifying creature. It looked rather like a lioness; it was the same tawny colour, perhaps a little darker. It had short, pointed ears, its eyes were set well forward in its face, and from its upper jaws protruded two long fangs. It was a giant cat; the sabre-toothed tiger, in person. It, too, had obviously been wandering through the domes when it caught sight of us and, very likely, was just as frightened to see us as we were to hear it roar.

"Don't move," said Jet, "don't anybody move."

The animal seemed to regard us with some curiosity. It stood still, emitting an occasional low purr from its throat, its tail lashing incessantly. It didn't come any closer, but remained half crouching, and staring. After a while it slunk to one side and then, with a bound, disappeared behind a dome.

Lemmy breathed an audible sigh of relief. "I thought we'd had our chips then," he said.

"I think he was scared of us at first," I said, "until he knew we didn't intend to harm him."

"If he'd chosen to attack us," said Mitch, "we wouldn't have stood a chance."

"Well, that just about establishes what period of time we are in," said Jet. "That thing couldn't possibly be in the future."

"And it also establishes," said Lemmy, "that we're not safe out here. We've got to get back into the ship and quick."

"Yes, I think we'd better. Come on."

Jet took a few paces forward, then stopped. There, in the city of domes, every one identical and equidistant from the next, it was impossible for us to have any sense of direction. We were lost.

"Now wait a minute," said Mitch, "which was the last building we looked at?"

"The one directly behind us," said Jet.

"No it wasn't," protested Lemmy, "it was that one over there."

"I'm sure it's this way," said Mitch.

"And I know you're wrong; it's this way." Lemmy pointed in the opposite direction.

"Now hold on," said Jet. "We'd better face it, none of us knows which is the right way."

"We shouldn't have come in so far," I said, "not without taking our bearings first."

"Well, there's no point in going any farther," said Jet. "Now, when we came out of the ship, did any of you notice which way the sun lay?

None of us had. We didn't even know at which point of the compass the ship was standing in relation to the city we were in.

"Maybe if we could climb to the top of one of these domes we could get high enough to see the ship," said Lemmy, "before it gets too dark."

"And what do we use for footholds?" asked Mitch. "It would be like trying to climb a wall of glass."

"Then what are we going to do? Stay out here all night with them tigers and heaven knows what else walking around and licking their chops?"

"Unless we find a way out of this maze, that's just what we'll have to do."

"Then how about calling up his nibs again? Maybe he'll reply to us this time and perhaps he can help us."

Jet switched on his radio but didn't even have to make the preliminary call, for out of his ear-piece we could all faintly hear the Voice:

"Hullo – hullo, Luna."

We all hastily switched on our sets and listened intently.

"Hullo," said Jet, "we can hear you."

"Why didn't you answer before?"

"We did call you, before we left the ship, but you never replied."

"No. We were too busy watching you."

"Watching us – do what?"

"Exploring our city."

"Then it *is* a city."

"Does that surprise you? Many forms of life all over the universe live in communities."

"But what's the idea of watching us?" asked Lemmy.

"Just curiosity. See how you would react to what you saw."

"All we did was get lost," said Jet in disgust.

"And meet a tiger," added Lemmy indignantly. "Do you know those things are hanging around here?"

"Of course; many other animals, too."

"You mean you let them?"

"Why not? They do us no harm, and we certainly do them none."

"But one normally expects a wild animal to attack you."

"Attack?"

"Yes, attack," repeated Jet. "Fly at you – kill you, maybe."

"Unless you kill him first, of course," said Mitch.

"The thought never occurred to me."

"Then how do you protect yourself from such creatures?" said Lemmy.

"They never bother us, nor we them."

"Oh, I see." Lemmy turned to Jet and spoke in a whisper. "They must look more horrible than we thought – even a sabre-toothed tiger is scared to go near them."

"Have you seen enough of the outside of our city?" asked the Voice.

"More than enough," said Lemmy. "We want to get back to the ship, where we feel safe."

"You are afraid?"

"Wouldn't you be in our place?"

"I don't think so. Animals are timid but you have no reason to be, because, unlike animals, you can reason."

"I don't see that that follows at all," said Lemmy. "It's just because I can reason that I know when to be scared."

"You must be more primitive, more backward than we thought."

"Now look, mate, there's no need to get personal," argued Lemmy. "You told us yourself we were in great danger. That's how you persuaded us to come here."

"To be in danger is not necessarily to be afraid."

"Look," said Jet determinedly, "whether we're scared or not we have no desire to remain here all night. Can you guide us back to the ship? At least we can stay there until morning."

"If you really wish it. But I was about to guide you somewhere else."

"Where?"

"To me."

"Oh," said Jet. "Is that far?"

"No."

"What do you say, Mitch – and you, Doc?"

"If we're going to end up with the Voice anyway," said Mitch, "we might as well go now."

"Yes, Jet," I agreed.

"All right," said our captain, addressing the Voice. "What do we have to do? Where do we go?"

"You see the dome in front of you?"

"Yes."

"Walk round to the other side."

"Just that – nothing else?" asked Jet.

"No, nothing else."

"All right, gentlemen," said Jet, "let's go."

I was convinced we'd walked round this same dome before; however, when we got round to the opposite side this time, we found a door. It was the entrance to a tunnel which sloped steeply down and was lit up for about twenty yards. There the light stopped and it was too dark for us to see what lay beyond.

The moment we entered, the door closed behind us. There was no turning back now. We walked slowly down the slope. As we did so, lights came on further ahead and those behind us went out so that only part of the tunnel immediately before and behind us was illuminated. It was an ingenious device, and once we understood it we continued on our way with more confidence.

We must have walked for an hour, our footsteps echoing round us as we made our way deeper and deeper into the earth.

"I don't think we're ever coming to the end of this tunnel," said Lemmy, wearily. "If it's like everything else in this place – built on a circular pattern – all we'll do is end up where we started."

"Hey, wait – stop a minute. See – there."

Jet pointed directly ahead. Before us in the darkness was a pinpoint of bluish light. "It looks just like an eye. Well, doesn't it?" he went on when none of us replied.

Lemmy gulped. "Now you mention it," he said, "it does."

"And it's as though it's watching us," I said, "staring at us."

"Here," said Lemmy, "do me a favour, will you, Doc?" Then, "Hey! That couldn't be the Voice, could it?"

"How can an eye be a voice?" asked Mitch.

"I mean *his* eye."

"Only one?" said Jet.

"Why not? If he's as different from us as he says he is, maybe he's only got one. Maybe that's all he is – an eye."

"How could an eye stay up in the air like that, with no support?" said Mitch disparagingly.

Jet switched on his radio. "Hullo – hullo," he said anxiously. "Can you hear me?"

"Yes," came back the Voice.

"We can see a light, a bluish light – very small and directly ahead. We don't quite know what to make of it."

"Keep walking until you reach it, and you will pass through it."

"What do you think we are," said Lemmy, "mice?"

"It will grow as you approach it."

"Oh, I see."

"Then we'll keep going," said Jet, "and thank you."

"It's a pleasure," the Voice replied.

"That's more than it is for me," said Lemmy.

Jet switched off the radio and we continued our walk in silence, each of us wondering what lay at the end of it.

Chapter 13
ESCAPE

W e caught our first glimpse of what lay beyond before we actually reached the outlet and we all broke into an involuntary run to get closer to the unbelievable sight before the vision faded.

But it was real enough.

There, a hundred feet or more below us, lay a vast plain. Like most things with which we'd been concerned lately it was circular. It was an immense garden, filled with flowering trees, but of shapes and sizes I had never seen before. They appeared to be akin to the cacti family but their blooms, while just as brilliant, were far more profuse. Gorgeous reds, blues, yellows, pinks, whites and purples were to be seen everywhere; it was as though the multicoloured clouds of a brilliant sunset had been snatched from the sky and laid on the earth. The trunks and boughs of the trees were the colour of red cabbage. Most of them were covered in scales like a pineapple and from each scale there projected a thin, pointed leaf, about two feet along and perfectly straight.

But the most fantastic thing was the sky. It was a delicate, pale blue and although it was impossible to tell where the light came from, its soft rays shone down to bathe the whole scene in a delicate warmth.

"It's all a dream," said Mitch, almost in a whisper. "It must be."

"Or a nightmare," said Lemmy. "A beautiful nightmare."

"It's daylight," exclaimed Jet. "How can you have daylight underground, at night? And the sky is ..." He paused and looked again. "It's not the sky," he said, "it's a roof. This whole thing is artificial – an artificial world laid out under the largest dome one could ever conceive."

"How does it keep up there." asked Mitch, his engineering instincts coming to the fore, "with nothing to support it? There must be millions of tons of earth above it; the pressure must be fantastic."

We stood silent for a while, enthralled by the majestic scene.

"Whoever built it," I said at last, "must have a great love of beauty."

Our reveries were finally interrupted by the Voice. "How do you like our home?" it said.

"Is this where you live, is this your city?"

"What is left of it."

"We'd hardly call this a ruin," said Jet, a trace of humour in his voice.

"No, not a ruin, but a city is not alive without inhabitants, and they are all gone, or very nearly."

"You mean you're going to leave all this behind?" I asked.

"We are taking specimens of every plant with us to our new home. We could not live without them. They supply us with food and keep the air fresh."

"But why do you live underground?" asked Jet.

"The climate of Earth is too violent for us to live permanently on its surface."

"Hm," said Lemmy, "they can't be as tough as we thought."

"Well," the Voice went on, changing the subject, "you'd better come down."

We were standing on a large platform, about twelve feet square, and running down from it were three very steep flights of stairs.

"Fall down that lot and you'd have a nasty bump," observed Lemmy. Nevertheless, we made our way down, finding the going difficult as the distance between the steps was just a little more than our legs could comfortably manage.

On reaching ground level, we discovered the trees were, on an average, about twelve feet tall and even the trunks of some of them were covered in blooms. The scent was almost overpowering, but strangely invigorating like fresh sea air. We began to feel good-humoured and quite cheerful again. We followed the path that led from the steps and wandered aimlessly along, intrigued by the purply trees, the multicoloured flowers and the dark-red soil.

Suddenly the Voice brought us back to reality. "Hullo," it said.

"Yes?" answered Jet.

"You are getting very close to me now. In a few moments we shall meet."

We were standing near where the path divided. One branch led to a sphere, a complete one this time. Instinctively we sensed that the Voice, whoever or whatever he was, was in it.

"Soon the door will open, but you needn't enter if you don't want to," the Voice said. "You may just like to look in."

"Very well," said Jet. We moved towards the sphere and as we did so a circular door near the ground began to slide open.

Fear took hold of Lemmy. "I don't like this," he gasped. "Let's go back."

"No, Lemmy." I spoke sharply. "We're staying right here." The door was completely open now.

"Can you see anybody – anything in there?" asked Jet.

"No," said Mitch. "It's rather dark, it's – yes, I can. There – see?" His voice changed. "Oh – cripes!"

We all gasped, for what we saw was indescribably horrifying.

There was too little light to reveal much detail and what there was seemed to emanate from the creature itself. It was about twelve feet high and was scaled all over with what appeared to be a kind of bright armour. Whether it was sitting or standing, I couldn't say, but its knees were bent and it was probably in a squatting position. Its arms – it had two – hung loosely at its side and the scales on its body were flashing in all colours, like luminous mother-of-pearl. But the most luminous and fearsome part of the thing was its face. It glowed in red and blue.

Lemmy took one petrified glimpse, then took to his heels, shrieking: "Let me get out of here." Jet immediately started after him, and in the moment Mitch and I turned to watch them the door of the sphere had closed again.

We looked at each other uneasily. "He must have seen how the sight of him affected us."

"It was a hell of a shock," I said. "Quite unlike anything I'd expected."

"He was like a – well – I . . ."

"An armadillo."

"Yes, I suppose you could describe it as that – armoured anyway. It stood up on its hind legs."

"And it had a blue and red face, like a – a mandrill."

"It was the bright colours that gave me the biggest shock. I expected somebody rather like ourselves, flesh-coloured, at least."

Jet returned with a protesting Lemmy. "What happened?" he asked. "Did the door shut again?"

"Yes, Jet – almost immediately," I said. "It was as though he wished to hide himself from us as quickly as possible."

Lemmy was almost whimpering. "Jet, let's go away from here."

"No, Lemmy. We mustn't let him see we're afraid."

"I'm not afraid, not any more," said Lemmy indignantly. "I just couldn't stand to see anything so ugly again, that's all."

"The sight of you had much the same effect on us when we first saw you," the Voice broke in.

"Eh?" said Lemmy.

"But we got over it and now we accept you."

"But we couldn't be that ugly."

"Quiet, Lemmy," said Jet urgently.

"It's all a matter of comparison, what you're used to – the habit of accepting what you *think* is normal."

"A fellow can't help his ugly mug," said Lemmy, "but you've taken things a bit too far."

"I'm sorry, but I did warn you. You need not see us again if you'd rather not."

"Thanks. I'd rather not," said Lemmy with finality.

"You must excuse us," I said, placatingly, "but you're so unlike anything we expected."

"We understand. You need worry about it no more. Now I expect you'd like to refresh yourselves and rest."

"Yes, we'd like to very much," said Jet.

"It has all been arranged. If you follow this path, you will come to another sphere, just like this one. Go inside. When you have rested, I will contact you again."

Lemmy, who had got over his fright and now seemed rather ashamed of his behaviour, said: "Thanks a lot. I'm sorry I kicked up all that fuss."

We found our 'lodging' without difficulty and entered the sphere by the usual circular door. Inside were four couches, a table with what appeared to be food on it, and a spherical televiewer by the wall. Otherwise the place was bare. Mitch walked over the table and picked up one of the platters.

"Do you think this is good to eat?" he asked.

"Only one way to find out." Breaking a piece off, I put it in my mouth.

"Well, what's it like, Doc?" asked Jet.

"Not bad," I told them. "Very sweet, rather like honey but with the texture of bread."

"And I suppose these things are for us to sleep on?" said Lemmy, going over to one of the beds and pressing it with his fingers.

"What else?" asked Mitch.

"What do we do for bedcovers?" went on Lemmy.

"Perhaps they don't expect us to undress. The Voice didn't seem to be wearing any clothes."

"Eh? What about all that shell stuff – that armour-plating – wasn't that clothes?"

"I doubt it," I told him.

"Well, I don't know about you," said Mitch, "but I'm hungry. I'm going to risk eating some of this stuff and then get me some sleep, bedclothes or no."

We'd soon consumed every piece of food in sight, including the sweet, rather sticky liquid that we found in a large container placed in the middle of the table. After we'd eaten, Mitch moved to one of the beds and lay down on it.

"How's it feel, Mitch?" Jet asked.

"Oh, quite comfortable," he yawned. "I feel so tired I could sleep on a clothes line."

"Are you warm?" asked Jet. "Hey, Mitch – " But he was sound asleep.

"Here," said Lemmy, "I suppose it is just sleep. That couch couldn't be some kind of trap, could it?"

"How could it?" asked Jet.

"Well, why not? You lie on it and – whoops, you're off, lost to the world. Then when all four of us are laid out, in come them gremlins or whatever they are and we've had it."

Jet walked over to Mitch and shook him. "Huh? What's the matter?" asked the Australian.

"Are you all right, Mitch?" asked Jet.

"Why shouldn't I be?"

"Well, we thought that . . ." He didn't finish, for Mitch had turned over and was fast asleep again.

"It's as though those beds made you sleep whether you want to or not," said Lemmy.

"But he woke very easily for Mitch," said Jet; "almost as soon as I touched him."

"I don't think there's anything to worry about," I said. "It seems the whole make-up of these people is based on gentleness and kindness."

"But how could anybody so ugly be so kind and considerate?" asked Lemmy.

"For the same reasons as anything so beautiful as a – a cat can be so cruel."

"That makes a kind of sense, Doc," admitted Lemmy.

"And sleeping makes sense, too," said Jet, lying down as he spoke. "I think you'd better turn in as well, both of you."

"Good night, Lemmy," I said as I stretched out on the third couch.

"What do you mean, 'good night'?" he asked. "It's broad daylight out there."

"I expect it always is," I told him. "But that won't stop me from sleeping."

I woke to find the bed hard, uncomfortable and prickly. I was glad to climb out of it. Mitch and Jet were already up and were standing over Lemmy, smiling as they watched him writhing.

"What's up, Lemmy?" said Jet. "Can't you sleep?"

"No, I can't. This bed's so darned uncomfortable," he replied. "It was fine when I first got in, but now it feels like a plank – a bare plank with splinters in it."

"That's just how mine was," said Jet, "and Mitch's."

"What's that human mandrill trying to do – make a monkey out of us?"

"Good morning," said the Voice. "I trust you slept well."

"I would have done, if the bed had stayed as comfortable as when I first got in it."

"But it did."

"Eh?" said Lemmy.

"You slept for hours. The beds don't get uncomfortable until you've had your full sleep."

"You mean they are some sort of sleeping pill and alarm clock combined?"

"What an ingenious idea!" said Jet.

We had awoken with a remarkable feeling of freshness, for our long sleep had done all of us the world of good. The tired, strained look had left Jet's face, Mitch was sweeter tempered and Lemmy less pessimistic. A bath or shower would have made my morning complete, but either the Time Travellers thought we had no need of such twentieth-century luxuries or they were not acquainted with aquatic methods of cleanliness. But they had not forgotten our breakfast. We sat down at the table and cheerfully ate a hearty, if somewhat monotonous, meal. We had hardly finished when the Voice called us again.

It wanted information about our ship, Luna – how it worked, what the motive power was, its maximum speed and all kinds of technical details which only Mitch could give. The enquiry went on for nearly an hour. Between them Jet and Mitch explained why it would be impossible for us to take off from the Earth and return to the Moon under our own power, and why it was impossible for us to take off at all while the ship remained in a horizontal position.

Finally the Voice said: "Now we are in possession of the facts, it is easy for us to see how the accident happened."

"Accident?" asked Jet. "What accident?"

"The one that brought you to your present position. It was never intended. But I think perhaps now we can get you off the Earth again, and back into space."

"That's wonderful," said Jet, his relief manifest in his voice.

"Could you leave in a few hours if your ship were ready?"

"Certainly," said Jet eagerly, overwhelmed, as we all were, at the prospect of going home.

"Then return to your ship," said the Voice, "and take off in the usual way. Climb as high from the surface of the Earth as your motor will allow, and leave the rest to us."

"I hope," said Jet, "that you don't intend to return us to the Moon. It will take about all the fuel we have to effect a take-off. Once we landed on the Moon, we would never get off again."

"We do not intend to take you back to the Moon."

"You'll leave us coasting towards the Earth, then?"

"No."

Jet looked a little puzzled. "Then where do you intend to take us?" he asked.

"To the planet you call Venus."

"To Venus?" Jet repeated. "Why to Venus?"

"Because that is where we are going."

The piece of honey bread I was chewing turned sour in my mouth. There was a hollow, sinking feeling in the pit of my stomach. Mitch, who'd been taking a drink from a shiny metal container, let the cup fall to the table from where, after spilling its pale-yellow liquid, it rolled with a clatter to the floor. Lemmy gulped. Jet struggled to remain calm, and it was some time before he spoke.

"You heard that, gentlemen?" he said quietly.

"I told you this was a trap," said Lemmy. "All this feeding us, these beds and everything – it wasn't kindness at all. It was just a trick to get us here and make us prisoner."

"But why to Venus?" asked Jet, almost to himself. "We'd die as soon as we set foot on the place."

"Why should you?" the Voice enquired. "You managed to exist on the Moon, and Venus is not nearly so hostile."

"But I don't want to go to Venus," said Lemmy. "I want to go home – to Earth."

"But you are on Earth."

"Back in our own time, I mean; in the twentieth century where we came from."

"That we can't allow."

"Why not?" asked Jet.

"If we take you back you will build other space ships and make further trips to the Moon and beyond."

"Of course," said Mitch. He could not suppress the note of fanaticism in his voice. "That's the reason why we started out on this trip in the first place. Man has a new frontier to conquer, the frontier of space. And nothing will stop him."

"Not even if every space ship that left Earth failed to return?"

"Oh, so that's your little game, is it?" said Lemmy. "You're going to lie up there on the Moon, waiting for ships to come out from Earth so that you can knock 'em from there into the middle of next week."

"How else can we prevent Man conquering space?"

"Why should you wish to?" asked Jet. "You've conquered it yourself, haven't you?"

"We had to leave our planet – we had no choice."

"I don't see that that makes any difference," argued Mitch. "There's no universal law to say that beings from one part of the universe should travel it at will while those of another should not."

"Our reasons are sound enough," said the Voice. "Perhaps, if you care to watch the televiewer globe, I can convince you."

We all turned towards the pedestal where it stood near the curving wall. Jet got up from his seat and walked round the table towards the glowing sphere, as did the rest of us.

"These," said the Voice, "are the forest creatures."

The picture was clear enough. It showed a group of men, if you could call them that; for they were men from a long forgotten age, men at their wildest and most primitive.

"Prehistoric men – our an-ancestors!" I gasped.

There were about ten of them, including women and children. So far as I could tell, they were neanderthaloids. Their skins were of a dark hue, whether naturally or from the want of a wash I couldn't say. Their hair was auburn, their noses flat and their eyebrows beetling. From their wide mouths, which frequently opened in a snarl, long canine teeth protruded. Their feet were broad and large and, as they walked, their arms swung like a chimpanzee's. Their bodies, as well as their heads, were covered with hair, thick and matted on the chest and thighs. The men had long ragged beards and some of the women held children to their breasts. They all carried some kind of weapon, either a long, sharpened stick, a branch of a tree shaped as a club, or merely heavy stones which they picked up from the ground and used as missiles. They were all stark naked and walked with a stoop.

"When we first arrived here," the Voice continued, "thousands of years ago, there were only a few of these animals. But they have steadily multiplied and emerged as

195

creatures with intelligence. They live in small communities and have learned to make fire. They have an insatiable desire to destroy us and all that belongs to us."

"Then why don't you do the same to them?" asked Jet.

"We can do many things, but we cannot harm any living creature."

"Well, that's a comfort," Lemmy said to me quietly.

"But won't you even kill for food?" asked Jet.

"There is no need to kill to live."

"But life is like that," argued Jet. "One animal kills another so that it may survive and that, in its turn, is killed by another. And so on."

"So we found when we first arrived on Earth; it was something new to us. But these creatures that you see have a far higher intelligence than any other animal and yet behave little differently. There is an incredible selfishness in their nature. They fight savagely for food and mates – even kill each other. They would kill *you* as soon as look at you."

"But they won't come looking for us down here, will they?" asked Lemmy.

"No. They seldom leave the forest."

"Then we've got nothing to be scared of, so long as we stay here."

"But you can't."

"Why not?" asked Jet.

"I've already told you. The last of us are about to leave, and we cannot protect you when we are gone. Already the forest creatures had begun to get curious about you. That is why we brought you here – where you can remain in safety until we can remove you to Venus to spend the remainder of your days in peace and comfort."

"That's what you say," put in Lemmy, "but how do we know what you might get up to when you get us there?"

"You don't have to come. You can remain here if you wish."

"With those gorillas, you mean?" said Lemmy. "And you say you've no wish to harm us."

"It would not be us that harmed you; it would be the forest creatures, your own ancestors."

"Ah! That's the point, isn't it?" said Jet. "You think that because we're descended from those – those cave men, we're still like them. That's the true reason you won't attempt to get us back to our own time."

"Can you blame us? We have seen the forces that drive them, their uncontrollable desire to destroy anything they do not understand. Can you imagine what such creatures would do if let loose on a peaceful planet where violence was unknown?"

"Yes, I can," said Mitch, "but twentieth-century man is not like that. We are quite different, you can see that for yourself."

"Physically, yes, but it takes a long time for such things to be driven out of a being's nature – a long, long time, longer than your kind has inhabited this planet."

"But in comparison with the age of the Earth," I said, "Man has hardly existed any time at all."

"You are merely proving my argument."

"But even in that time we have learned a lot," said Jet. "We've progressed."

"You mean you don't kill each other any more? You no longer destroy the things that can give you life and comfort, as the forest men burn our crops which they could eat if they knew how? You are certain that the instinct does not remain in some other form?"

Jet was silent. "Look," he said at length, "we're not perfect. I don't know how long your kind has been alive, probably many thousand times longer than Man. You've had time to conquer your primitive desires, suppress them. You have endless generations of experience behind you. Give us the time and we'll be like you. We'll stamp out the undesirable part of our natures; but you must give us the time."

"I realise that," said the Voice. "But meanwhile are you to be allowed to expand into the realms of space; to destroy others, perhaps? To conquer space before you have even conquered yourselves?"

"You can't help destruction of some kind," said Mitch. "You can't plant a field without you clear the forest first. You can't drive a steam engine without you dig out the coal or pump out the oil from the bowels of the Earth."

"Oh yes, you can," said the Voice. "There is power all around you; forces for all to use, with no digging and no pumping, no waste."

"We haven't learned to harness that power yet," said Jet. "We don't even know what it is."

"Then perhaps you will leave your exploration of space until you do."

"But don't you see," Jet was emphatic, "that is where you can help us."

"How?"

"By telling us your secrets."

"Would you explain the workings of your ship and all its equipment to the forest creatures?"

"What would be the point?" asked Jet. "It would be like trying to explain the quantum theory to a child."

"Exactly."

But Jet was not to be defeated. "At least," he said, "you could make a start – with simple things. We are not quite as primitive as those ape men, even by comparison with you."

"A child cannot be taught to run before it can walk, and you have hardly emerged from the crawling stage."

"You don't think much of us, one way and another, do you?" asked Lemmy.

"We think as much of you as we do of any other living creature anywhere in the universe. We have no wish to harm you."

"But if you leave us here," said Lemmy, "it amounts to the same thing."

"For our own safety, for the safety of our generations to come, it would be better to leave you here – to prevent your ever going out into space again."

"Then you don't know us as well as you think you do. Our deaths would make no difference. Man will conquer space; and neither you nor anybody else will stop him."

There was no reply to Jet's last remark. We stood in silence and watched the cave men on the screen. Some of them were now sitting on the ground. Two were fighting, tearing at each other's throats with their fingernails. Others gathered round them, snarling and growling as though they, too, were likely to join in the fight at any moment. Then the picture faded and the globe became opaque once more.

Jet called the Voice two or three times but got no reply. So, one by one, we wandered back to the table and disconsolately sat down.

"Well," said Jet, "what do you think they'll do now?"

"Take us to Venus, of course," said Mitch. "What else? How can we prevent them?"

"We don't have to take off," I said.

"I suppose they could find a way of making us if they wanted to," said Lemmy. "I wouldn't put it past them."

I wasn't of Lemmy's opinion. "I don't think they would ever make us do anything against our will," I told him. "The worst that could happen would be for us to have to leave this city and make our own way through this hostile, prehistoric world until death overtook us all."

"Blimey," said Lemmy, half smiling, "we wouldn't half put some of those archaeologists in a flutter if they found our skeletons in the same grave as one of those gorillas."

"Well," said Jet, "we'd better decide what we want to do. If they insist on taking us to Venus and no other place, are we to accept or not?"

"No," I said decisively. "At least we know we can breathe the air here. And, with luck, we may keep ourselves alive for some years yet. On Venus we might not live five minutes."

Mitch disagreed flatly. "If it comes to a final choice," he said, "I think I would go to Venus."

"Good heavens, Mitch," said Jet. "Why?"

"For the same reason as I went to the Moon. If I'm never going back to my own time anyway, I might as well see as much of the universe as I can before I die."

And so began a lengthy discussion – hours of argument broken by long silences or walks outside to breathe the deeply-scented, invigorating air.

I was outside the sphere when I heard Jet call me. I ran back into the globe to hear the Voice saying, "We have decided, against our better judgment, to help you get back to your own time."

We were immeasurably relieved. "Thank you," said Jet quietly.

"Wait. We will help you, but there will be a considerable risk."

"We don't mind," Jet spoke for us all, "if there's a sporting chance."

"We may not land you back at exactly the same time as we first picked you up. Are you willing to take that chance?"

We were.

Two hours later we were aboard a Time Travellers' saucerlike ship, watching a 3-D reproduction of the country we were travelling over as it passed through the spherical televiewer screen. The journey as far as the river was uneventful. Then, just before we were due to land, we saw from the televiewer that our transfer from the time ship to Luna was not going to be easy.

The first intimation of our new peril was a dense cloud of smoke rising above the forest in the direction of the river. A few moments later, as we sped on our course, we saw that the cultivated fields were burning furiously. Lining the river hank were swarms of ape men.

"What the devil are they up to?" asked Jet anxiously.

"It's pretty obvious, isn't it?" I answered him. "They've set fire to the fields, as the Voice said they frequently do."

"Is it just the fields," asked Mitch, "or is it something to do with our ship?"

A closer study of the televiewer told us what he meant. There was Luna all right, but a change had come over her. Instead of resting on her undercarriage as we had left her, Luna was standing on her tail. The ladder to the now highly elevated cabin was extended and the main door open.

Clouds of smoke were drifting by her and at first we thought that she, too, was surrounded by the flames. But although an attempt had been made to burn the grass round her, it had not taken well and was now only smouldering. The flames were emanating from the nearby crops.

There were about a dozen ape men and women quite near to Luna, and when they saw us coming they took to their heels and ran – but only for about a hundred yards, then they turned to watch us complete our descent. They must have realised long ago that the time ships never harmed them.

The moment we landed the televiewer picture dissolved and the hatchway in the ceiling slid open.

Jet climbed the ladder first, the rest of us following closely behind. The dome was already open when we reached the upper deck and we paused at the entrance to survey the scene. There wasn't a great deal to see because of the smoke that was drifting past. So far as we could tell, the group of cave men who had been near the ship when we landed were at least a hundred yards away, but there might be others, much closer.

"If only we had a gun," said Mitch. "A spear – anything – we would at least have a chance to defend ourselves – if they decide to attack us."

"You mean you'd kill them?" I asked him.

"If it came to it," Mitch said, "yes, I would."

"But you daren't," I said.

"Huh?" Mitch looked at me as though I were crazy.

"How can you? These people are our ancestors. For all we know, each of us is directly descended from them. If you kill even one, you might well kill a child as yet unborn and his children and his children's children, and so on down to the twentieth century."

"Good Lord," said Jet. "It hadn't occurred to me. To kill one of these people might change the whole course of human progress and civilisation, and if we do get back to our own time, we might find the world is a completely different place."

"We might well," I said.

"Then what are we to do?" asked Lemmy. "Supposing they kill us?"

"That won't matter," said Jet. "We are not the past. Nothing they do to us can affect it. It could only affect the future. But God knows what havoc we might do if at this stage we wipe out something of what has been. There's nothing for it but to try to reach the ship before they catch up with us. If they do attack, we must try to avoid harming them. I'll go first, and the moment we're all safely in the lock, we'll retract the ladder. Is that clear?"

We all assented and without another word Jet made his way towards the ground. I was the last to go and by the time I'd touched down Jet was already sprinting towards Luna, and had covered half the distance. Close behind him was Mitch and then came Lemmy about twenty yards in front of me. The smoke was still thick. It got into my eyes, making them water and difficult to keep open. Half choking and half blind, I ran as hard as I could, following the swiftly moving Lemmy.

I think I must have been within ten yards of Luna when it happened. Close to my ear there was a half-roar, half-scream, like the raving of a lunatic, and the next moment I felt a hot, steel-like grip on my shoulder. I tried to wriggle from the thing's grasp, lost my balance and fell to the ground with the beast on top of me.

I was so terrified that for the first second or two I was completely paralysed. I had fallen on my back and was now staring into the most horrible face a 'human' being could have. The whites of his eyes were bloodshot and the creases in his skin were engrimed with dirt. As his mouth opened, drops of saliva fell on to my face and I could see his yellow, decaying, fang-like teeth. His long hair hung about his eyes, and his reddish, bushy beard, which, even then, I could see was full of vermin, hung to within an inch of my own face.

He had the strength of a horse. As soon as I was under him, he reached for my throat as though to tear it apart. I grabbed his wrists and exerted all my strength to deflect them from their savage intent. As I did so, he began to snap at my face like a dog. His breath stank noisomely. I began to yell at the top of my voice for help. At the same rime, I brought my knees up and put my feet into the pit of my adversary's stomach. Then, gathering all the force I could muster, I pushed. This most elementary ju-jitsu must have been a new experience for him. He crashed on his back a good three yards beyond me.

I gave him no time to recover. Even as he was rolling over, I was up on my feet and running towards the ship. Almost immediately I ran slap into Lemmy who, hearing my cries, had turned round to come to my aid.

"Go back," I yelled. "It's all right now. Go back."

I must have looked terrified, for Lemmy, after one glance at my face, stepped aside shouting: "After you, Doc. You go first."

I didn't argue, but made for that ladder as fast as my legs would carry me. I could hear Lemmy panting behind me as my hands grasped the rungs and I began to climb towards the airlock.

"Hurry up, Doc," said Lemmy. "He's right behind."

I didn't dare turn round until I had climbed the first few rungs and given Lemmy the opportunity to put at least his own height between his feet and the ground. Then I looked back, to see the ape man who had attacked me making a clumsy attempt to follow us up the ladder.

"Don't stop, Doc," yelled Lemmy. "Keep going." I kept going. By now Jet had reached the main door and, holding on to the side, was leaning out of it, yelling encouragement at us in our desperate climb. Mitch wasn't far behind him. Suddenly I realized that Lemmy was not following me so closely. Again I stopped and looked back. He was some thirty or forty feet above the ground, and the ape man was slowly but surely coming up behind. But to my horror Lemmy, instead of climbing, was now descending.

If Lemmy heard Jet or any of us yelling at him, he took no notice but continued his descent until he was only two rungs or so above the ape man's head. By now there were three others gathered at the bottom of the ship. Lemmy waited as the ape man advanced another rung, and then another. And then I realised what he was up to. Almost as the thought occurred to me, Lemmy went into action. Letting himself down almost to full arm's length he began energetically stamping on the ape man's fingers. The creature let out a series of cries, like a dumb man trying to talk, and then, with a piercing roar, he went crashing down on to the heads of his companions below.

Lemmy began to climb again rapidly and less than thirty seconds later we were all in the airlock and Jet was passing through the cabin hatch to the ladder control. There was a whirr as he pressed the switch and the rungs slid back into the ship, leaving the wall smooth and unclimbable. In spite of this, the creatures down below, including the one who had just fallen, still tried to find the rungs and went through the motions of climbing on the spot.

Lemmy and I were breathing very heavily. I turned and put my hand on his shoulder. "Thank you, Lemmy," I said.

"Forget it, Doc," he replied. "Let's get up into the cabin and get away from here."

We closed the hatch, closed the main door, emptied the airlock, climbed onto our couches and, with our control panels already in position, strapped ourselves in. Soon the televiewer was warm and Jet had Lemmy rotate the forward view towards the sky. As we waited for the Time Travellers to appear, I filled in the last few pages of my diary. A quick check-up within Luna had revealed that not only was everything restored to order – in line with the information Jet and Mitch had given the Voice – but we had even been supplied with food and drink for our journey.

"Those Time Travellers certainly must work fast," said Mitch. "How they ever got the ship into this position, I'll never fathom out."

"They must have had dozens of men on this job," said Lemmy. Then he stopped himself. "Men?" he went on. "What am I saying?"

"I have no idea how they did it without us," I said, "but I think I know why."

"Why, Doc?" Jet asked me.

"Because, after the way we reacted, they didn't want us to see them again."

"It makes you feel so mean, doesn't it?" said Lemmy. "We can't stand the sight of them and yet they do all this for us."

"They're an amazing people and no mistake," said Mitch.

"After this," Lemmy went on, "I wouldn't care if I saw a hundred of them. And if I did, I'd shake hands with the lot – if they have hands."

"See if you can contact them, Jet," suggested Mitch. "We must thank them."

"Yes, Jet," I said. "That's the least we can do."

But at that moment there appeared on the screen twenty spots of silvery light. The Time Travellers were waiting.

Perhaps the rate of climb was not as strong as it had been when we first left Earth or perhaps, by now, my body had begun to get used to the varying acceleration rates we had experienced since leaving home. Anyway I hardly noticed the pressure as we climbed towards the sky.

Eighty seconds later the motor was cut and we were coasting up, out of the atmosphere and into space. On Jet's order, the rear televiewer was switched in, and we could see the time ships behind us, once again flying in the crescent-shaped formation and peeling off as though to attack . . .

EPILOGUE

"That's all there is, Jet," I said as I closed my journal. "It stops there."

"Do either of you remember anything about what Doc has just read?" Jet asked Mitch and Lemmy. Neither of them did.

"But I did have a feeling we'd been round to the other side of the Moon before," said Mitch.

"I had much the same feeling myself," I told him, "but as for what's in this diary, it's all new to me."

"But if what you've written is true, it would account for the fuel and oxygen shortage."

"And for the food being all different," added Lemmy.

"They'll never believe this back on Earth," said Jet. "I can hardly believe it myself."

"They'll either think we're plumb crazy," said Mitch, "or we cooked the whole thing up as a practical joke."

"Hang on a minute," said Lemmy. "I've got an idea." And with that he went over to the food locker and began rummaging inside it. A moment later he came back to us, his face beaming.

"Here," he said, "what about this?" It was the stone knife; the very one described in the diary.

Jet took it from Lemmy and turned it over in his hands. "Good heavens," he said, "then it must be true, every word of it. We would never have picked up a thing like this on the Moon."

"But we could have brought it with us from Earth," said Mitch, "to substantiate our story – or Doc could, anyway."

"Mitch," I said slowly, "are you accusing me of fixing the whole thing up?"

"Why not? The newspapers back home would pay a lot of money for this sort of story."

"Now, wait a minute," interrupted Jet. "Nobody's fixed anything."

"Then how can you prove it?" said Mitch sarcastically.

"I don't know," said Jet. "Many strange things have happened in the five weeks since we left Earth. I don't see what further proof you need."

"We could start digging under the Mediterranean – see if we can find the ruins of that underground city. Very convenient that where we are supposed to have landed is now covered by thousands of feet of water."

"Lemmy," said Jet suddenly, "call up Control."

"Call up Control?" said Mitch. "What for? To be laughed at?"

"No, Mitch, to tell them we're short of fuel and may have difficulty landing. We'll look deeper into that diary and all that's connected with it before we breathe a word to anybody at home."

"Now you're talking sense," said Mitch. "If we're not careful, all the reception we'll get will be from a bunch of psychiatrists."

At that moment Lemmy contacted base and called Jet to the control table.

"Hullo, Earth," said Jet, "this is Morgan speaking."

There was a short pause and then the familiar voice from Luna City replied.

"Hullo, Jet. Everything OK? You're dead on course, we're plotting you all the way."

"We're out of fuel," said Jet flatly.

"What?"

"Yes, and landing may be a bit tricky. It's most unlikely that we'll be able to use the motor."

"Well, if you handle her right, you can glide in; you've got bags of room. The whole Outback is at your disposal."

"I just can't guarantee to put her down on the launching ground. You may have to go out into the desert and look for us."

"Don't worry, we'll be ready. We'll send a fleet of helicopters out the moment we know you've touched down."

"Good," said Jet.

"Anything else?" asked Luna City.

"No, nothing else – not at present," said Jet. "What news have you got? Anything big been happening back home?"

"No, Jet. You're the biggest news we've had for years. Oh – until this morning."

"Why? What happened?"

"There's been another flying saucer scare. The biggest we've had since the 1950s."

"Saucers?" exclaimed Jet.

"Yes," came the voice from Earth, "and sighted over Australia, too. By a dozen independent eye-witnesses. They were flying too high for anyone to notice any detail – they always are. But there were supposed to be about twenty of them altogether and flying at tremendous speed in a crescent formation. Only half an hour after being seen from Australia they were sighted over America. So you'd better watch out for them, Jet. Maybe they're trying to steal your thunder."

Jet turned from the radio control to glance at Lemmy, Mitch and me who were standing behind him. Then he turned back to the microphone.

"Yes," he said slowly "we'll look out for them. We'll call you again in a couple of hours. And thanks, Control – thanks a lot."

It was less than two hours after I had read my diary to the rest of the crew that the news of the saucers came over the radio from Control. It was then that I decided that this account of our adventures, based both on the remembered and 'forgotten' events recorded in my diary, should be written.

Since then four and a half days have passed and we are now close enough to the Earth to attempt a landing. Already Jet has gone into the pilot's cabin and taken his place at the controls. Whether our glide landing will be successful is an open question – I think we have a fifty-fifty chance.

Meanwhile I shall put this book in the food locker – and place the stone knife on it. It will be safe there and well protected in case the worst should happen.

Jet has ordered us to our posts. I must go . . .

fantom
publishing

Charles Chilton
JOURNEY INTO SPACE

Between 1953 and 1958, millions of people tuned in to the radio adventures of Jet Morgan and his crew as they left Earth to investigate the universe. Chilton went on to write three best-selling novels based on the groundbreaking radio series.

OPERATION LUNA   ISBN: 978-1-78196-024-0

Destination – the Moon! No adventurers had ever faced greater hazards than the crew of rocket ship *Luna* when she hurtled into space. Jet Morgan, ace pilot, was her captain. With him were her Australian designer, Mitch; Lemmy, the Cockney radio operator; and Doc, whose diary astonished everyone.

THE RED PLANET   ISBN: 978-1-78196-025-7

Blast Off! to new heights of adventure and excitement with Jet Morgan and the crewmen of the spaceship *Discovery* as they lead the first fleet of rocketships to reach across space to the 'Red Planet', Mars. But right from the beginning the expedition seems ill-omened. Uncanny happenings test their courage to breaking point, both on the long space flight and on the hostile planet itself.

THE WORLD IN PERIL   ISBN: 978-1-78196-026-4

An alien civilisation prepares to conquer Earth – and only four men can save her... Jet Morgan and the crew of the *Discovery* return to Mars on the most dangerous and vital mission ever undertaken by man – to obtain the Martian plan for the conquest of Earth. Too late, they find themselves part of the invasion fleet.

Available in paperback from
www.fantomfilms.co.uk

Also available from

fantom
publishing

AUNTIE'S
CHARLIE

AN AUTOBIOGRAPHY BY
Charles Chilton

Described by the *Sunday Telegraph* as 'the one genius the BBC ever had on its staff', Charles Chilton MBE joined the Corporation at fifteen as a messenger boy and went on to carve out a 46-year career as a presenter, writer and producer.

Auntie's Charlie tells of his life from growing up on the streets of 1920s St Pancras, via early years at the BBC working for the Gramophone Library, to writing the infamous production *Oh What a Lovely War* for Joan Littlewood's Theatre Workshop.

While with the BBC Charles was sent to the United States to research, write and produce a number of series based on American western history. One of these, *Riders of the Range*, lasted for five years until 1953. However, major international recognition came with his science fiction trilogy *Journey into Space* which he wrote and produced between 1953 and 1958.

Here, for the first time, is Charles Chilton's story in his own words – an autobiography that is frank, vivid, wry and engaging.

Limited edition hardback ISBN 978-1-906263-72-0
Standard edition paperback ISBN 978-1-906263-76-8

Available from
www.fantomfilms.co.uk

Also available from

fantom
publishing

THE
HAMMER OUT
BOOK OF GHOSTS
2012

A collection of short ghost stories published in aid of

Registered Charity 1102750

Foreword by Tracey Childs, actress and patron of Hammer Out

Established in 2002, Hammer Out was set up as a small fundraising group to raise awareness of brain tumours and the needs of those affected by them as well as raising money for brain and cancer related charities. All profits from the sale of this book will go to the charity to help fund research, raise awareness and provide support for people suffering from brain tumours and their families.

This volume includes stories by Paul W.T. Ballard, Alex Barrett, Niall Boyce, S.E. Branson, Raven Dane, Jan Edwards, Simon Guerrier, Richard Howard, Louise Jameson and Sam Stone.

ISBN 978-1-906263-58-4

Available in hardback from
www.fantomfilms.co.uk